UNLIKELY STORIES

UNLIKELY STORIES

T. R. McCay

The Fast Plates
The Salamander
Gort's Butt

Edited by
Karen Tarleton Holland

WorldCraft Publishing
4080 Veselich Avenue, Los Angeles, CA 90039 USA
www.WorldCraftPublishing.com

WorldCraft
DREAM, WRITE, SHARE

I wish to dedicate this book to my original campfire captives: my darling wife Bonita, Tim Powell, Stan Richeson, Nate Powell, and Jim Daw (a.k.a."Imaginary Jim"). I would also like to express my profound thanks to David Castro and Mickey Lawler. Without all of you, I would be living under a bridge writing stories on cardboard boxes.

T. R. McCay

Contents

Forward

T. R. McCay is a walking encyclopedia of knowledge: paleontology, chemistry, metallurgy, history — world, local and military. Folklorist, backpacker and survival skills expert. Science fiction author, part-time soldier, accomplished chef and restaurateur, chemistry lab tech, backwoods foot surgeon, welder, and weapons expert — with experience in most modern and historical weapons.

Have a question about any ship, weapon, battle, historical figure, or obscure piece of trivia buried in layers of sedimentary rock? He has an answer, a name, a chemical analysis, and a hundred-odd bits of trivia to go along with it. If he doesn't have an answer, he'll tell you so and go find one. He can't help it. He's a consummate storyteller. He has the Gift.

T. R. McCay and I met when he was four years old and I was three, and have remained the best of friends since. Our families knew each other socially, we occasionally visited his family-owned restaurant that specialized in slow-smoked, southern, mustard-based, pulled pork barbeque, which remains the standard to which I've always held all barbeque. By default and circumstance, like his father before him, he also became a master of the craft.

McCay is the best backpacking partner one could hope for. He taught me how to savor the silence only a forest can bring. Taught by his Daddy Roy, he naturally knows things when it comes to the great outdoors: where to find dry firewood in the rain and snow, find clean water, and how to avoid injuries. How to pick a campsite and the best gear. He taught me early on to always leave a campsite better than you found it. He's notorious for breaking up "unauthorized" fire rings and intimidating lazy scout leaders who've let their charges run slip-shod over the protected wilderness. He taught me the Canine Mystique. And, yeah, he cooks. Really well.

I first heard his Southern-flavored speculative fiction stories around a campfire, six-or-eight miles from the nearest paved road. After a grueling 10-or-12-mile push, following a great McCay fire-cooked supper, he pulled out a wad of crumpled yellow legal pad pages and said, "Boys, I got somethin' here I'd like ya'll to hear. Any feedback is welcome." And then proceeded to blow our minds as he read to us *The Salamander*.

At first, Stan, Imaginary Jim (if he was even there), and I were all skeptical and somewhat trepidatious because we were, in actuality, trapped. Hell, he'd just fed us, and we were stuffed and weary. It's cold, dark and scary in the woods all alone. We couldn't escape, so we listened. And we were amply rewarded. Transported, even. As I'm sure you will be as well.

Tim Powell

Preface

Years ago, across from the main Broadway entrance to Columbia University in New York City, there was a bookstore named Papyrus. Papyrus wasn't very big. They didn't sell toys or greeting cards. They didn't do coffee or snacks. There was no place to sit or go to the bathroom. Yet Papyrus was worth more than a thousand of today's warehouse paper dumps. I tried to hit Papyrus every payday.

All the authors I had grown up reading were there. Asimov, Bradbury, Clarke and Heinlein. There were hundreds of other Science Fiction authors, perhaps not as famous but nonetheless brilliant: Simak, Farmer, Lem, and this uppity word machine named Stephen King. At Papyrus, there were multiple feasts unknown. All you had to do was come in and join in. It was like going into the abyss and flipping on the lights. Suddenly you're surrounded by fantastic creatures few others would ever see or even suspect. You could gorge yourself on alien worlds and alternative realities like a polar bear chowing down on a walrus. It was at Papyrus that I caught an incurable infection. I wanted to be a writer too.

The years flashed by at Mach speed. I could never shake the writer's bug. At first, I wrote in secret on yellow legal pads. Then, not so secretly, I discovered that being a writer was like a miner working a creek for gold. Every now and then, you would find a few flecks of placer washed down from some unseen and unknown source. Never anything to pay the bills, but just enough flecks of gold to keep you going.

I caught the bug at Papyrus, but it was around the campfire that I learned to tell the story. Humans have told stories around the campfire as long as humans have controlled fire, but it's only when you actually do it that the advantages become obvious.

After a long day on the trail, all that most people are able to do is eat something and zombie out around the fire. This is important. This condition means they are too tired to run away no matter how lame the story is. When you're backpacking in a remote wilderness, fleeing into the darkness is ill-advised. It is just a lot safer to sit there and listen to me.

The three stories in this volume — *Fast Plates, The Salamander,* and *Gort's Butt* — are those original campfire stories.

T. R. McCay

The Fast Plates is a story about a fella who finds movies and unknown technology from the American Civil War. Here, grifter Jimmy Broadfoot's shady past intersects with an unknown, long dead genius. Does Jimmy take a giant payout, or for once in his life, does he do the right thing?

The Salamander is more than a cautionary tale of why you should never backpack alone. It is about the two invisible worlds that are present in every moment of our lives. The first world consists of the memories between our ears. The other world is the vast unknowable, just beneath our feet. Between them, the protagonist has an encounter that is as harrowing as any alien abduction.

Finally, there is the story of *Gort's Butt.* If you are a science fiction fan, you know that Gort was the incredible robot from *The Day the Earth Stood Still*. You might also know the words to calm it down. Every time I watched the movie, I felt like it was only half the story. In *Gort's Butt*, humanity accepts the alien ultimatum. It should be the dawn of a golden age for humanity. There are no more wars, poverty, hunger, crime, or massive environmental violations. You would think it would be all peaches and cream, but as I've already said, nothing is simple.

THE FAST PLATES

The Fast Plates

For once in my life I'm going to be completely honest. I'm no angel but I'm no devil either. With only a handful of exceptions, anyone I ever grifted was happy with his end of the deal, but that's not unbelievable when you think about it. Everyone who has ever drawn breath and walked the dirt of the Earth, for better or worse, believed in just what suited them. When most people hold a piece of history in their palm, all they see is a dirty lump of brass and want to wash their hands. But some romantic souls, knowing that this is a time-encrusted button from a British grenadier's coat, will act like they got a piece of the True Cross. Sometimes they will place their treasure in a glass case and show it off to friends like a snappy car or a hot new girlfriend. Sometimes they will hide it in a safe, only releasing it late at night so they can gloat over it like a miser croons over a stack of gold coins. So essentially, it just depends on your point of view. There are some people, some of them quite well off, who will go to just about any length for the experience. For a collector in Virginia it might be a last heart-wrenching letter home the night before Manassas.

If you can get the knack of mimicking nineteenth-century penmanship, vocabulary and phraseology, those are pretty easy, but like counterfeit money, no matter how good the work, you'll get caught if you put too much out there.

I began to discover this when I started to occasionally fake my parents' signatures on a few marginal math tests, and once, even a report card. It wasn't because my grades were that bad; I did it for fun, just to see if I could get away with it. My folks were so busy they never noticed anything. Finding out I could do it for money made me one very happy sixteen-year-old. My bogus signatures were perfect, but it was too good to last. Inevitably, someone ratted me out, and I got a spot on that hot seat they keep down at the principal's office. Assorted adult authority figures blustered, foamed and threatened for an hour, citing violations of school rules, educational ethics, and God's law. Of course, my folks stood up for me, but I knew they suspected the truth. In the end, the authorities had to let me go. They couldn't prove shit and we all knew it. Everyone has a talent for something, even if they live their entire lives without discovering what it is. When I walked free that day, I knew what mine was. Like relativity, it was a discovery with far-reaching consequences.

It was the first life lesson that I took to heart: when lying, stay as close to the truth as possible. It's a dogma that has served me well.

Buttons, ammo pouches, belt buckles, horse tack, and sword hilts all require period brass and sometimes even a little gold. Lucky for me the people who made the original regimental buttons and doo-dads used the same stock for casting door knobs. And the stock even had an agreeably low melting point. A few months interred in a flower pot full of acidic soil and you've got a winner. My hobby turned profession with an entire set of "recovered" Confederate general officers' brass buttons "salvaged" from a highway construction site near Vicksburg and sold to a European collector. When you add up the time and trouble of locating originals, palling around with the little old ladies that run small community museums, surreptitiously making copies, positives, and wax negatives, casting, and aging the artifact, it almost makes me want to get a real job. Sometimes I think it would probably be easier to steal Jeb Stuart's hat, but not quite; you always have to consider the love of what you're doing.

I only had one job that went sour enough to be nearly fatal. It was an engraved sword hilt, with part of the blade still attached, that had belonged to Captain Andrew Ambrose Mahoney, an officer of the ill-fated Irish brigade whose remains had never been recovered. Allegedly found during the excavation of a new gas pipeline near the aging Marye's Heights above Fredericksburg, the sword hilt was a triumph of craftsmanship, but not of research. To my delight, it sold for a shockingly high price to the Bostonian, Peter Flynn, who claimed to be a direct descendant of the gallant Captain Mahoney. The man was thrilled, and I was happy he was happy.

My problems began when he didn't stay happy. I have no idea what made him suspicious. He might have reflected on the odds against such an amazing coincidence and decided they were a little too long. Maybe he had found out there had been no gas pipeline. Whatever tipped him off, it wasn't long before he found that the steel blade had probably come from a circular saw made in the 1920s, exposed to the elements for many years, then etched with a weak solution of nitric acid. Isotopic analysis revealed the gold used in gilding the hilt had been mined in the Johannesburg district of South Africa. In my defense I would like to point out that the grip and hilt were drawn from my collection, therefore absolutely authentic. The problem was that it was a pattern manufactured thirty years after the Civil War in the final days of old-fashioned cavalry.

You wouldn't think a Boston big shot like that would have gotten his panties in such a twist over ten grand. Hell, he spent more than that adjusting the local cops every week. If I had handed the cash back over to his boys when they came to collect one early Sunday morning, I probably would have gotten off with a stern verbal warning. But seeing how I had already gone through most of the money, they just took it out of my hide, my car, my single-wide, and my reputation. The Bostonian told any collector who would listen, and my whole carefully constructed livelihood came down like a sandcastle at high tide. I suppose I was lucky to have a fallback career, but it takes a trainload of scrap iron to pay for a new set of front teeth.

I've never been good at keeping a regular job, but Buck Horton didn't care about that. Buck didn't care about a lot of things. When I turned up, he wasn't put off by the sutures in my upper lip or the busted headlights on my old Mustang. He just sat there puffing on a hand-rolled Prince Albert and asked me if I could operate a cutting torch and drive a D3 bulldozer. I answered in a painful lisp.

"Of courth, Buck, you the man who taught me how."

They say that home is any place where they have no choice but to take you in. In my hour of need, I had returned to Fort Scrap and thrown myself at the commandant's feet, begging for mercy like a common deserter. Buck had accumulated a lot of things in life, but mercy had been ditched in France back in 1918. I could have come crawling through the bald-tire gates of the county's biggest scrap yard wearing nothing but dirty long johns with an ass full of arrows and he wouldn't have cared less. Buck just needed someone to cut up junk cars and strip the copper out of dead refrigerators for slaves' wages.

Of course, I was a little special. I might not have been the son that Buck never had, but I was as close as he was ever going to get in this life. Buck had nabbed many a copper thief prowling the chaos of Fort Scrap. The lucky ones were picked up by deputies after they were dumped in a weedy ditch down the road. The unlucky ones were never seen again. Sometimes, older and bolder kids would scale the black steel-belted radial tire walls on a dare. Buck caught them like bluegills with cherry bombs, sending them home with striped legs and tear-streaked faces, and somehow he always got away with it. Buck didn't have a junkyard dog and didn't need one. Buck was the junkyard dog.

He caught me one Saturday afternoon trying to steal a gun. There was a schoolyard rumor that Buck tied one on each and every Saturday, and if you wanted to get in and snoop around, that was the time to do it. I did it on impulse and out of boredom. If that day had been sunny instead of rainy, I would have been mowing yards instead of scaling the tire wall at the back of Fort Scrap.

I'll never forget my first sight of Fort Scrap when I hauled myself over the wall and squeezed through a gap in the barbed wire. Vehicles of every imaginable description as far as the eye could see. Derelict cars, wheelless wagons, and crumpled aircraft were piled haphazardly into a range of rusty hills covered with kudzu and poison ivy. There was a lot to explore: rows of three-wheel postal jeeps waiting for their turn in the smelter, and mountains of tractor tires awaiting execution in an industrial grinder. But the thing that piqued my interest was a collection of old Quonset huts clustered in the middle of the yard.

Quonset huts were the brainchild of some government bureaucrat tasked with housing millions of new soldiers and their equipment in a great big hurry. Picture a galvanized sheet metal pipe thirty feet in diameter and sixty or seventy feet long. Now cut it in half lengthwise and plant one half on a concrete pad. Slap walls and doors on either end, dig a latrine out back and voila! — instant barracks. Buck had a couple dozen dilapidated units he bought after the Big One (WWII) for two cents on the dollar and installed on a foundation of plain red dirt. They were mysterious and alluring, as irresistible as an abandoned Roman outpost. I just had to know what was in them.

I got into the first one through a pair of misaligned panels and was disillusioned to find it only contained hundreds of old mattresses that smelled strongly of mice droppings and mildew. The next one was stacked with molding hobnailed boots and rotting wool overcoats, and home to thousands of tiny white moths. One hut that had me scratching my head was crowded with fifty-five-gallon drums filled with black rubber spheres about the size of ping-pong balls. By that time it was getting late and I was getting uneasy. The longer I was around, the greater the chance of being discovered by the owner. There are few things I hate more than a burnt run, so I decided it was worth one more effort to find something worth stealing.

The next hut was almost buried under heaps of kudzu and poison oak, but I spotted an opening staring at me like an empty eye socket. It was all the invitation I needed. When I got in, I just stood and stared for a long time, listening to the rain tapping like skeletal fingers on the curved steel roof. I had hit the jackpot. It was filled to the roof with stacks and stacks of guns. There were bundles of bolt-action rifles, rifle barrels, rifle stocks, barrels of spent brass, bins of paralyzed pistols, piles of doughboy helmets and canteens. Obsolete radios and switchboards were piled against the curved steel walls, along with enough sabers, saddles, and horse tack to outfit a regiment of cavalry. It was a quartermaster's nightmare, everything crusted over with a fusion of time, grease, dirt, and neglect. For a thirteen-year-old boy, it was the next best thing to a warehouse full of naked horny women with a sexual fetish for myopic adolescent boys. The only problem was deciding what to take. I was so absorbed in the exploration of this incredible discovery that I didn't notice when Buck slipped into the hut.

He was like that; the old fart could sneak up on a pack of police dogs. I had no idea how long he had been watching me. I just suddenly smelled booze and stale piss, looked up from a barrel of deactivated hand grenades, and there he was, silhouetted against the opening where I had crawled in. He gripped a long hickory switch in one hand and an almost empty bottle of Four Roses in the other.

"Whatcha doin' in here, boy?"

I just stood there looking stupid as he took the measure of me. He slowly set the bottle down on an anonymous wooden crate and flexed the switch between his hands. Buck was big, dirty and drunk, looking me up and down like a Turkish prison warden analyzing a fresh fish. Then he smiled his toothless smile and stepped forward, obviously intending to teach me a lesson on the hazards of trespassing. I was as stuck as a rat in a rain barrel. The only way out was past Buck and the hickory switch. What I did next might have been the reflex of desperation or just too many John Wayne movies, but I had no intention of just standing there and letting some old drunk stripe my legs like I was his own half-wit kid.

I grabbed a gun off the nearest stack of surplus weapons and hefted it to my shoulder. I remember it like my first piece of tail. It was taller than me, a trapdoor Springfield rifle-musket with a cracked stock and a bent barrel full of cobwebs. For some reason, its bayonet had been left fixed to the muzzle where it had been fused into place by a hundred years of corrosion. Buck came up short and stared at me, trying to focus his drunken eyes in the gloomy hut. Slicing the air with the switch, he started forward again and I cocked the hammer. The action felt like it was packed with dirt dauber nests, but it locked with a menacing metallic click. I pointed the old fossil at Buck's head and he stopped cold in his tracks. I announced my intentions and demands in the cursedly cracked voice of puberty.

"You come one more step and I'll shoot!"

He scowled, grunted, and took a step forward with the switch poised to slash me in the face. I pulled the trigger. CLANK. His mouth dropped open in a mix of shock and disbelief.

Looking back on that moment, it's not hard to understand why. The old piece of junk hadn't been fired since Grant was president. My chances for success would have been better with a matchlock. I cursed the worthless weapon for all I was worth and let out my best growl.

"Get the hell out of my way or I'll stick you like a bullfrog!"

Buck began to laugh. He laughed so hard that tears rolled down his cheeks. He laughed so hard he wet his overalls. That really hurt my feelings. He threw down the switch and sat down on an ancient wooden ammo box so hard the wood cracked under the stress, almost spilling him onto the dirt. This made him laugh even harder, rubbing salt into my already lacerated sense of manly dignity. Now I was the outraged one. I flourished the cruddy blade in a demonstration of my serious intent and got a little too close to the old guy. He moved with the speed of a cobra, springing up and grabbing the musket just behind the blade and wrenching it away before I could blink.

He stood there, suddenly stone-cold sober, the weapon held rock-steady and pointed right at my face, the bayonet's still-lethal tip about six inches from my nose. He wasn't laughing anymore; he looked cold and detached like he could run you through with a spear and then sit on your corpse for a smoke break. Normally I would have started to weep and plead for my life but fortunes had reversed so quickly, I didn't have time. Buck smiled and lowered the musket, giving me a knowing look.

"I just as soon you didn't, kid. Getting poked with a bayonet hurts like hell."

He tossed the musket back onto the pile and produced a can of Prince Albert and a grimy pack of papers from the bib of his overalls. He began to calmly roll a lumpy cigarette that didn't look at all like the ready-made smokes my dad used.

"What's yer name, kid?"

I felt a little more at ease, a little more principal's office, and a little less bayonet-wielding drunk.

"Jim."

He licked the paper and appraised me with watery blue eyes.

"You got a last name, Jim?"

"Yes sir. Jim Broadfoot."

He blew on the damp paper.

"You William Broadfoot's boy? Got the hardware store?"

"Yes sir."

Buck nodded and handed over the hand-rolled cigarette.

"Smoke, Jim?"

I grinned. "Don't you think I'm a little too young to smoke?"

He shrugged his boney shoulders.

"Shit fire, you old enough to bayonet a man, you old enough to smoke."

It was still wet with slobber; I blew on the paper like he had done as he rolled another. He finished and fished around and pulled out a small brass tube. The cap swiveled off to reveal a striker and wick. He flicked the wheel and a bright yellow flame leaped up.

He held it toward me.

"Light?"

That's how I met Buck Horton and began to develop a lifelong struggle with addiction to nicotine.

The years flipped by as I cut up everything from river barges to giant transformers sold off by the TVA. Two or three times a week a grimy tractor-trailer would come rolling in like Charon with his boat and back into an angled pit in the center of the yard. Then I would shove tons of steel into the dented rig and it would all be hauled away to the afterlife of recycling. Not bad work for a kid who wasn't even old enough to drive.

A boy could have made more from a paper route, but the *Birmingham Mercury* didn't provide free smokes. Besides, my folks thought it was safer hanging out with Buck than riding my bike around town in the predawn darkness busting out windows with rolled-up newspapers. We even had kind of a uniform: greasy overalls, hobnailed boots, green pith helmets with a faded Marine Corps emblem, and cheapo mirrored sunglasses. The dozer was so old it had steel cables instead of proper hydraulics. The left track tended to stick in reverse if you weren't careful or even if you were careful, and the only way to fix it was to get into the gearbox and bash away with a ball-peen hammer. I loved her like my first Mustang. The best part of the job was that Buck let me have pretty much anything that struck my fancy, and I fancied quite a bit.

Dusty old sabers brought a whopping seven dollars apiece, or two for ten. The trapdoor muskets — two dollars a pop, bayonets not included — weren't good for anything but frightening small children. Anyone dumb enough to fire one with anything like the original charge was liable to lose an eye or a few fingers, but guys liked to hang them over the mantel and concoct stories about them. My great epiphany came when, on pure impulse, I sold the bones of a Remington single-action revolver, impulsively claiming I had found it on the banks of the Tennessee River just below Pittsburgh Landing. It had really been recovered from the trunk of a crashed '49 Desoto coup, but just the mention of Shiloh increased its value to my first glorious Ben Franklin. I even threw in a display case for free. I had found my calling in life, or at least it was until I got caught and had the crap beaten out of me by a Hibernian goon squad.

Buck had never looked what you would call well, but he had always had a sort of primal indestructibility about himself. When you caught him at just the correct level of drunk, he was more fascinating than pitiably obnoxious. Buck Horton was a man who had had more close calls than Adolf Hitler and had plowed more pussy than Casanova. Buck had been kicked by mules, chased out bedroom windows by outraged husbands, and fought hand-to-hand with the Kaiser's finest, shrugging everything off like a mild April shower. It was something too tiny to see that changed him into the man I met in the Quonset hut. They put him into a ward of hopeless cases with the rest of the doomed, but the sturdy little bastard refused to die. Every tooth in his head rotted out, a peculiar effect of the 1918 flu, but as always, Buck survived when the men around him perished like flies. By the time he had gotten back stateside, both he and his home had changed beyond any recognition. He had briefly been declared dead and returned to find his widow already engaged to another man. She had taken one look at this toothless gas-scarred wraith and walked away. He had inherited a fragment of worthless farmland located five miles out of town next to the city dump, and it was here that he established his own tiny nation, Fort Scrap.

The last time I saw Buck Horton alive, he was sitting in his rocker on the back porch overlooking his rusting, rat-infested empire, sipping on a mason jar of his own moonshine. Every drag off one of his nasty home-rolled smokes resulted in a coughing fit strong enough to induce a hernia. The network of tiny blue veins crawling over his face had vanished under a ghastly grey pallor. Puckered scars left behind by the mustard gas on his neck and ears gave him a sickly yellow halo. Molecules of the hellish blister agent were beginning to surface after seventy years like rats jumping a doomed ship. When I couldn't get him to relate the story of banging the living daylights out of a French general's wife, I knew he was in a bad way. I begged him to let me take him to the emergency room. I was so desperate that I offered to pick up the tab even though I didn't have enough money for an oil change. Buck shook his unwashed head.

"Thanks but no thanks, Jim. Come check on me tomorrow morning. I'll either feel better or I'll be stone-cold dead."

I knew Buck and I knew that was that.

I found him the next morning, still sitting in his rocker, an empty gallon jug of shine next to him on a cable-spool table. A large circle of charred cloth in his lap marked the moment of death. A live man won't willingly allow a cigarette to burn itself out on top of his genitals, but a dead one will. In one hand he held a picture I had never seen or expected to see. It was smiling young Buck with a mouthful of healthy teeth, in the high-collared wool uniform of a doughboy, arm in arm with a stunning black-haired woman wearing a wedding dress. I saw something in his other hand and pried the cold fingers open to find a bit of faded ribbon attached to a blue and white enameled cross. It hadn't been bullshit. Buck had been awarded the coveted Croix de Guerre by the grateful people of France. Something pinged on the floor, rolled under the rocker, and came to a rest leaning against a lifeless foot. I stooped down to retrieve a very plain wedding band as new and shiny as the night they were wed. Buck had had everything, Buck had lost everything, and now I had lost Buck. I sat on the steps and cursed God for being so unfair and moped around the place for an hour or two. Then I called the ambulance to come and collect the body.

I hate funerals. This of course is a normal reaction, but it's not just the loss that I find depressing. It's the bland farewell that goes along with the American way of death. No fireworks or real oratory or towering funeral pyre burning the deceased right back into the carbon from whence he or she came. No blood sacrifices to smooth the transition followed by a gigantic feast for the living. Just the brief display of a wax dummy that bears only a passing resemblance to the deceased, sent down to the underworld with a few off-key hymns and generic prayers. Buck's funeral was worse than most. I had requested burial with full military honors, but seeing how I wasn't even related, I wasn't authorized to do so. The request had to be made by a living relative or official guardian. Buck's only living relative was a grand-niece he had never even met, but everything he had processed in life would be passed to her. One look at this girl and I knew I was cut out of anything.

Chronologically she was about twenty-five, but on mileage she looked closer to sixty. Low-quality tattoos crawled over her skin like some inky sign disease, a counterpoint to a face full of metal posts and rings, apparently inserted at random. She hadn't even shown up for visitation but turned up for Buck's send-off ten minutes late, towing along a villainous-looking hollow-eyed boyfriend dressed in black leather. It was a graveside service in a cold drizzling rain attended and conducted by four people, while, at a discreet distance, a couple of backhoe operators waited patiently by their yellow machine like jackal-headed gods. The ceremony was short and to the point. As we were walking back to the cars, I attempted to introduce myself and was rebuked in no uncertain terms. Fort Scrap would be sold off to a developer, and if they found me there when they came back, I would be arrested for trespassing. When they drove away I was the one laughing hard enough to wet my pants. Buck claimed he hadn't paid taxes since about 1949, and I had no reason to doubt that was true.

In any event, I had absolutely no claim to Fort Scrap or even any right to be there. The charming couple who would inherit the old dump claimed New Orleans as their home, and I had it on good authority they were headed back south that afternoon. I didn't know how long they would be gone but was fairly confident the couple would party down over the weekend and return to find a lawyer who would begin sorting everything out next week. They might be back as early as Monday, no later than midweek for sure.

Whatever I was going to get for myself would have to be gathered up over the weekend. I arrived at the gates of Fort Scrap early Saturday morning to discover the sheriff had been there first. A bright red placard condemning the property was already nailed to the unpainted front door of Buck's shack, backed up by fluttering ribbons of crime-scene tape blocking the main entrance.

I went around the back to scale the tire wall at the very same spot I had infiltrated on that long-ago Saturday when I was thirteen years old. I sat on top of the black ramparts for a few moments looking for trouble, then eased down into the compound. I hit Buck's shack first. Buck might have been more than a little slack with personal hygiene, but his living quarters were neat and simple, almost spartan. His single bed was smartly made, the worn wool blanket tucked so tightly on all four corners you could bounce the proverbial quarter off its brown surface. The walls were innocent of any family photos, but there was a portrait of FDR, marked "Property of the US Postal Service."

His work desk had a sort of organized chaos: jelly jars full of pencils and dead ballpoint pens contested for space with car part catalogs and file folders stuffed with bills of sale. I found an unlocked cash box in one bottom drawer containing bundles of two-dollar bills and a few rolls of Mercury dimes. It totaled up to exactly two hundred ten dollars, which begged a question. The man had done a fair business over the past seventy years. I should know; I had been there to see a good bit of it come through the front gate and then go back out.

Buck sure as hell hadn't spent it on himself. He had no girlfriends and had never shown the inclination to rent one. He drank the cheapest rotgut on the shelf when he wasn't swilling down his own moonshine. Buck never took vacations and rarely went to the grocery store. He didn't even buy ready-made cigarettes, preferring Bugle Boy or Prince Albert in a can. One thing I knew for sure was that Buck hadn't lavished cash money on his single employee. I distinctly remember that the biggest sum he had ever forked over to me in a single week had been sixty-three dollars, and that had been only a week before he had died. Buck had to have money here somewhere and I only had about forty-eight hours to find it.

Buck's refrigerator was right out of the great Nixon-Khrushchev kitchen debate — a lime green monolith with about thirty pounds of chrome trim. It didn't contain the first scrap of food. I started with the freezer compartment. I found it packed tight with old-fashioned ice trays. I had never seen so much as an ice cube in anything Buck ever drank, so that made me suspicious. I pried one of the top trays loose with a large screwdriver and held it under a stream of warm water in the bathtub. It was only a few minutes before I spied a telltale gleam. Ten minutes later I held a string of gold class rings. I melted down the rest in Buck's grimy underutilized tub and came up with a couple of pounds worth of Masonic medallions, wedding bands, crosses, and even a Star of David, all gold, and a few with semiprecious stones.

It was a respectable haul, still way short of what should be here, but a fair start. A thorough search of the rest of his living quarters came up with nothing but trading stamp dishes and enough dried pinto beans to outlast the Siege of Leningrad. I sat on the back porch in Buck's rocker and tried to put myself into his second-hand shoes.

My mind wandered. I had always been bugged by the amount of crap we had around the place that never moved on down the line. Sometimes it takes a while, but sooner or later everything goes. Scrap is like any other kind of business inventory: you don't move it and pretty soon you go belly up even if you do dodge the tax man. On a hunch I cranked up a salvaged mine detector, held my breath and went into the old Quonset, still full of discarded mattresses from only providence knows where. Mice skittered across the floor as I forced the door open against an accumulated combination of cotton stuffing and mouse crap. The first nasty old mattress I tried came up empty, but the next pass over its neighbor rewarded me with an optimistic chirp.

I sliced open the filthy striped ticking, poked around with my switchblade and felt the unmistakable clink of metal on metal. The prize was an 1899 Morgan silver dollar wrapped neatly in brown butcher paper. I worked the mattress graveyard until I had scanned every bed in the warehouse while trying to ignore the squalid history written in unpleasant stains. The total take in face value was seven hundred nineteen dollars in silver, plus a cherry twenty-dollar gold piece. Not a bad day's work, plus Buck would have wanted it this way.

Weighed down with enough gold and silver to make Blackbeard happy, I went out the way I came, and very carefully drove home in the pre-dawn darkness. I was a little late on the tag renewal. The last thing I needed was a cop wondering where I came by a trunk full of bank bags stuffed with hard currency and jewelry. I made it home without incident, got some sleep, and spent most of Sunday cleaning and sorting my loot while I debated the risk of going back. Of course there was only one realistic decision. I went over the top after dark with fresh batteries and empty bags.

I didn't find much more — a water-damaged box of old porn magazines of indifferent quality, a few jars of wheat pennies, and

Buck's bankbook. I went right to the bottom line and laughed. I might not be able to get at it, but there wasn't much to get at. I decided that I had found my fair share.

Only Buck knew what he did with his money and he took that knowledge to the grave. On the way out I was skulking past the Quonset where I had been nabbed by Buck, and ducked in for sentimental reasons. There wasn't much left but crumbling leather shoes and a small mountain of old ammo crates stacked on a thin platform of pierced steel planking. The old telescope tube was still there, badly dented and with every lens cracked or missing. I had never been able to interest anyone in it. You can find people who'll buy old guns that won't shoot, but it's a little harder to find people who'll buy a blind telescope.

I had busted open a few of the crates years ago but hadn't found anything but a few scraps of paper and gunpowder residue. This would be my last chance at Fort Scrap, and I decided I would make the best of it. I dug through several layers of flat pine ammunition crates, prying open one after another, only to find a box full of stale air. I was getting a little discouraged when my light flashed across something different. I knew at a glance this was more than a box used for bullets, or in a pinch, an ad hoc latrine. I pulled away more of the pine boxes to find six large, grimy cubes, each roughly the size of an old army footlocker. I saw some traces of lettering. Wiping away decades of dust with my bandana, I found a completely legible name and address.

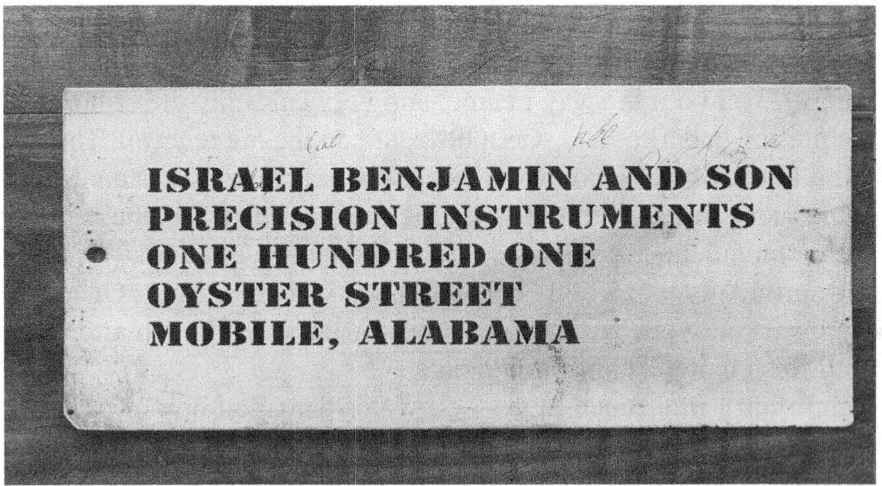

The lettering was in that blocky style favored in mid-nineteenth-century America. A damn good sign. I gave the smaller case a tug away from the rest; it was heavy but not impossibly so. It was good tropical hardwood completely free of rot. Even if it was full of rocks, the mahogany was worth something. Closer examination showed the box hadn't been nailed shut, but rather sealed with heavy brass screws. I found another larger stencil on the opposite side that didn't do a thing to enlighten me as to the contents. In large bold letters, it announced:

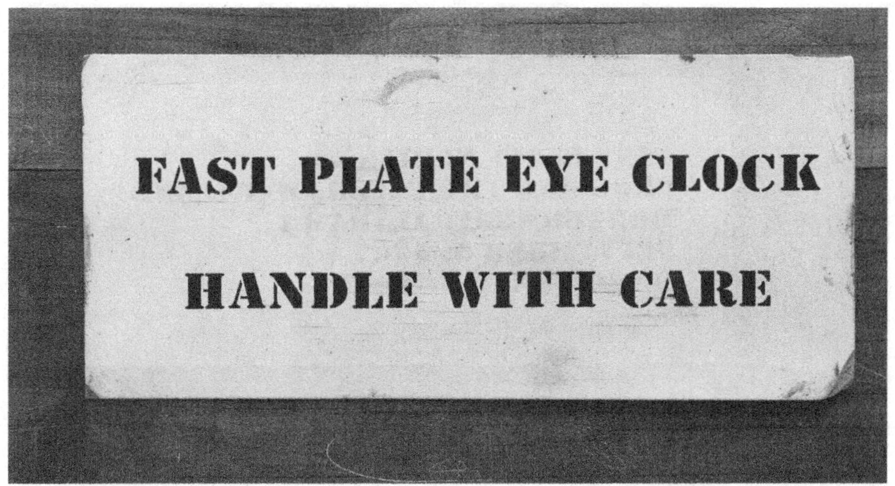

I carefully removed the screws and placed each one in my pants pocket. The top came off without cracking; the inside was stuffed with finely shredded wood shavings used before foam peanuts and bubble wrap to protect delicate items. There were no signs of nesting rats or any other vermin, another encouraging sign. Pulling out layers of packing, I found a black silk cloth covering a bulky object.

The desiccated fabric cracked and tore as I lifted it away to reveal another wooden box. I got closer with the light and saw it wasn't just a box; there was an angled slot covered with glass on one end and a broad lens the diameter of a teacup on the other end. I saw the dull surface of black iron. I groped around and came out with a small crank. It was a miniature version of the type used to start early automobiles, only a little more elaborate.

I couldn't decide if an eye clock was a telescope, microscope, camera obscura, or what, but I did know Monday was coming fast and I'd better get my ass in gear. I hastily replaced the top and went to one of the larger cases and tried to pull it away from the wall. It wouldn't budge. Placing myself between the hardwood crate and the steel wall of the hut, I braced my back and shoved with both feet. The case stubbornly grudged me a few inches. Now I could see lettering that had been hidden. I smeared away the grime and read the stencil.

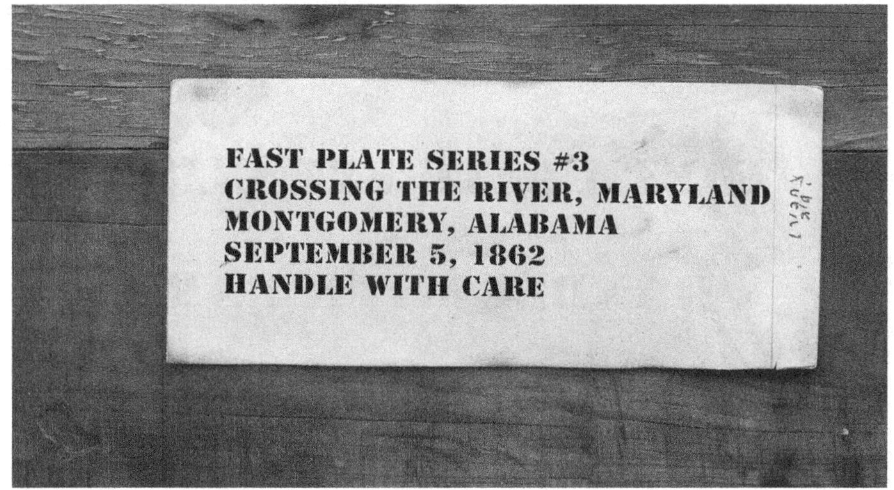

I followed the advice, opening the box like it was full of sweaty dynamite. More brass screws countersunk into heavy tropical ironwood, more shredded packing, and another layer of cloth that had once been a high-grade red silk. There, resting in its custom-built home, was a large brass cylinder lying on its side. I tilted the heavy drum up with difficulty and heard the clink of glass. There were convenient holes at intervals on the outside, just right to put your fingers into. Once I had a good hold, I muscled it out of its case, then eased it down on a loose section of steel plank. The inside of the cylinder was divided into numerous slots, each one containing what looked to be a rectangular plate the size of my hand. I tried to ease one of the plates out but it was wedged tightly into its own slot. I worried with it for another few seconds before it came free, then held it up in the light of my headlamp. I could make out some kind of darkened image, but it was hard to tell what. I took off the headlamp, backlit the glass plate and stared at it for a long time.

At first, I flatly refused to believe what I was looking at. I replaced the plate into its slot and pulled out its neighbor for examination, then another and another. I put the last one back into its slot with the same kind of care shown with a cranky blasting cap, sat down on an empty ammo box, and tried to absorb what I had found.

It had been waiting there for years, at least since the late 1940s. It had been there, only a few feet away the day I broke in and Buck had captured me. It had been there all the years I had worked for Buck and raided this very same hut for rust-pitted sabers and impotent trapdoor Springfields whenever I needed a few dollars. The most priceless discovery in American history had almost been dumped in a landfill, but by the grace of God, I had found it first. I had always suspected the reality of destiny, but now my suspicions had been confirmed.

The first concern was how to get the find loaded up and far away from here. Each case weighed nearly a hundred pounds, and just waltzing out the front would be risky. I could go through the back wall but that wouldn't be a piece of cake. Burrowing through stacks of worn-out tires filled with dirt wasn't practical unless I had something to give me an edge. Walking to the door I could see the old Caterpillar hibernating in its shed. I considered just crashing through the back wall if I could get it started, but that led to a host of problems. The area had become progressively more and more built up over the last few years. Cow pastures and peach orchards were rapidly giving way to strip malls and rental storage. The old yeller cat was loud as Judgment Day and smoked like a blazing oil rig. Then I noticed the solution hanging in the shed behind the bulldozer.

All I had to do was make a hole big enough to shove the cases through. I hitched one end of the chain to a power pole and hooked the other into the rim of a bottom tire. I began to ratchet the handle on the come-along, one stiff click at a time. The slack went out of the chain and the tire moved slightly. I prayed Buck hadn't reinforced the wall with rebar; my supplications were answered by a cascade of red dirt. The tire came out as the ones above it held their position. I had to dig and pull for an hour but was finally rewarded with a clear way out. I hand-trucked each case across the yard, eased each one as gently as possible over each bump and rut, then shoved each of them through the hole. Then, like any competent thief, I covered my tracks, shoving the tires back into place and covering my work from the outside with brush.

I drove away shortly after dawn with the old Mustang loaded to the limit. The rear end sagged low enough to produce a horrible screech against the pavement when I eased into my driveway, but I had made it. I pulled around behind the single-wide and backed up to the barn. It was the lone survivor of the old farm's original buildings, but it still had a good tin roof and solid oak doors. I parked the Mustang in the barn and walked toward the trailer, constantly looking over my shoulder, half expecting sheriff's deputies to come crashing in any second. Nothing but the morning song of a mockingbird and the hum of distant traffic. I returned with some cold fried chicken, a couple of celebratory Budweisers, a sleeping bag and pillow, and my mom's old .38 tucked into my back pocket. I ate dinner and then got mildly buzzed as I cleaned the grime off the cases and took inventory of what I had. I unrolled the sleeping bag in one of the old stalls and was asleep the minute my head hit the pillow. The hard lump of the pistol cushioned under my head didn't bother me in the least.

I woke up with a tremendous crick in my neck and the sun high in the sky. I went to the trailer, did my business, and dared to take a quick shower while the coffee perked. Every few minutes I'd peek out the window looking for trouble, but nothing had changed. The barn door was still locked and the grass still needed mowing. Back in the barn, I sat on the trunk of the Mustang for quite a while just looking at the tarp-covered cases, almost afraid to look at what I had found. Reviewing the inventory convinced me this was no fraud. It was far too elaborate and way too difficult to fake economically. The big question now was whether the eye clock still worked, if it ever had. I'm pretty handy with ceiling fans and bathtub valves, but one look at the guts of the eye clock had me pleading with the Almighty that it still worked.

Out of its box and on the workbench, I could really appreciate for the first time what a thing of beauty the eye clock was, even if it didn't work. Four feet long, eighteen inches at the beam and twenty-four inches deep, the casing was all tongue and groove, fitted together by someone who definitely knew what he or she was doing, probably a furniture maker. It stood on four small bronze lion's feet, the size of your big toe. The only other external decoration was an engraved silver plate tarnished with years but still legible.

The inside had a few flecks of green corrosion but nothing serious. I cleaned off the glass components with an eyeglass cleaning cloth dipped in a bit of Windex and picked away the few spots of verdigris with a dental tool. Finally, I had done everything I could think of to bring the ancient machine back to life. I inserted the iron crank into a recessed metal plug, obviously built to accept it, and gave it gentle forward pressure. It didn't budge; there wasn't even the slightest play in the mechanism. I jiggled and applied a few more drops of oil, wiping the small excess away with a paper towel, then gave it another try. Nothing. I examined the inner mechanism carefully for a loose gear or missing push rod but there was no obvious problem; it all looked to be in good condition. After pondering the difficulty for a few moments, I gave the crank an experimental pull toward me. The handle revolved smoothly and I could hear a muffled rhythmic clicking inside the case. Looking in as I turned the handle, I could see a busy assembly of cams, rods and gears, all working together in harmony.

Now I had a particle of insight. It takes a southpaw to know a southpaw, and one or both of these boys had been left-handed. Once I understood that, things went a little smoother. I fiddled and diddled with the eye clock until I could think of nothing to do but give it another whirl and see if I was the luckiest man in the county or just a self-deceiving idiot. I decided to begin at the beginning.

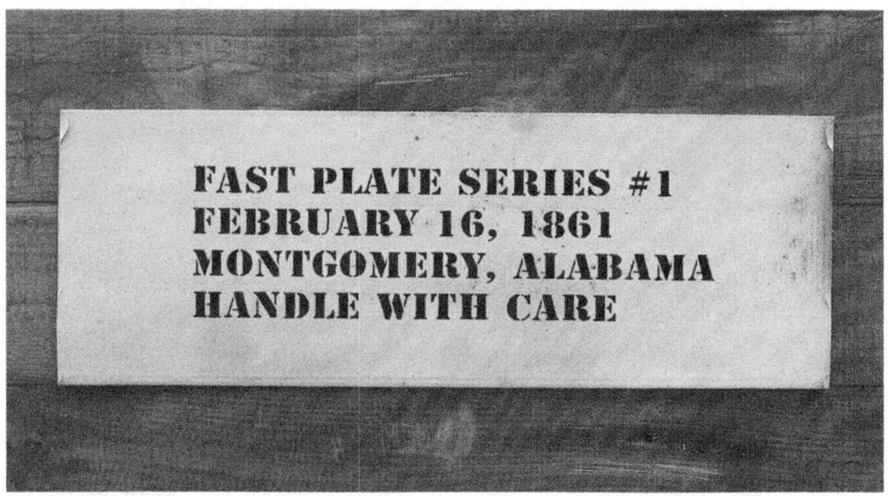

It was exactly like the ones I had already opened: shredded softwood packing, contents kept clean by a silk cloth slowly degrading into course red dust. The drum was exactly the same: a heavy brass framework with individual slots for each glass player, cushioned by thin strips of wood. Registration marks were thoughtfully provided and the whole assembly nested precisely on a pair of gears centered on the axis of the drum. I latched the top of the eye clock closed, placed my eyes against the viewer, took a deep breath, and turned the crank. I could hear a soft regular clacking inside the eye clock and the crank turned smoothly, but there was nothing to see but murky shadows. That one didn't take so long to troubleshoot.

I studied the teacup-size lens for a few moments, then began to dig around for a work lamp. I propped the hundred-watt bulb as close as I dared to the lens, plugged it in, and flipped on the switch. Another deep breath and a few hasty prayers, then I leaned forward into the viewing slot and began to turn. A vanished era leapt back into life — on an occasion that would result in the deaths of over half a million men and alter the course of world history forever. The grain of the image was a bit coarse and had a few black specks and fleeting scratches, but nothing much worse than an old *Keystone Cops* episode.

The loop began with a huge gathering of people crowded around the front of a palatial building with broad steps and classical columns. The men were dressed in black coats; most had already removed their tall black hats. The women were dressed a bit more festively, with long skirts and jaunty bonnets, all wearing gloves, some with their hands thrust into fur muffs. At the top of the stairs, two men, backed by a line of dark-coated troops at present arms, stood behind a podium. One was of average height with a shock of white hair, bright against his dark clothing. The other, tall and rawboned, black coat and vest over a white shirt with a high collar. He had badly groomed hair and a Billy Goat beard, and even from a distance you could see a grim determination etched on his angular face. His right hand was on a thick black book held out by the other man. Both men raised their right hands in the air, then the images looped back to the beginning.

This was no fake. No movie studio in the world could reproduce this moment with such accuracy. I knew exactly where it was. I had been there on several school field trips. I knew exactly who that tall man was. He had lived to the advanced age of eighty-one and had his picture taken more times than the Grand Canyon. The location was what is now the steps of the Alabama State Capitol in Montgomery. It was the inauguration of Jefferson Davis, the first and thankfully last president of the ill-starred Confederate States of America. I hadn't just discovered the first movies ever made; I had discovered movies from the early 1860s. I ran the loop one more time against my stopwatch — fast plate run time of exactly thirty seconds. At one-hundred-eighty plates per drum, this gave the whole shebang a blistering six frames per second, just enough to trigger the persistence of vision.

Now, I grant that even a modestly sized production company could reproduce the scene of the inauguration with a high degree of accuracy. But they can't really reproduce the people. No matter how much makeup and authentic costuming, there's a certain air about the subjects that defies duplication. Look at Lee's famous "Boots and Spurs" portrait. The uniform is magnificent, but if you study it closely, it also looks like something his mom made for him. That's because it is handmade and embroidered. Look at the man's hair; he looks like he just rolled out of his bunk after an all-nighter at the officers' club. Like most other photographs of people taken during that era, he looks hard, tough, determined, and a little mean.

That was a good way to be in 1860. Hot showers were unknown and baths were weekly affairs, if at all. Women oiled their hair to keep down the lice and literally used old rags during their periods, boiling them afterward in an iron kettle for the next month. Seeing how most families didn't have much in the way of consumer goods, you don't want to know where the soup was cooked. A puncture from a rusty nail could kill your ass graveyard-dead inside a week. Just like mumps, measles, scarlet fever, typhus, dysentery, or a bad tooth. If you crapped in the house you used a charming piece of functional ceramic known as a thunder mug, the contents to be dumped later in a hole in the backyard. You wiped your butt with corn cobs and washed everything, including yourself, in raw lye soap. It was a life fraught with dangers all but forgotten in the modern world. You didn't want to get injured back there.

Removing the drum I selected a plate at random and put it on an old light table originally used to read X-rays, last used to fake up nineteenth-century letters. I placed my best loupe in my best eye and took a closer look at the backlit plate. Davis was halfway through raising his hand and looking intently into the judge's eyes. The honor guard wore dark coats, which would probably be correct. Early in the war, many Southern units wore the old blue uniforms of the National Army. One Alabama regiment had gone into action at the Battle of First Manassas wearing the old uniforms, and had the shit shot out of them by both sides. You could see a number of women, but with one exception: their faces were obscured by bonnets. The one woman I could see had her face turned two-thirds toward the camera like it was more interesting than the swearing-in ceremony. She was young but completely innocent of makeup, giving her a very plain visage with inky circles under her eyes. The men had mostly removed their hats; all had appalling haircuts.

Like any great discovery, it all raised more questions than answers. I had never heard of Israel Benjamin and Son, but they had a Mobile address. Even if it was one hundred thirty years out of date, it was a lead. Whoever they had been, they had overcome formidable technical challenges. One of the challenges was a flexible medium to print the images on. Plastic, even flexible celluloid, was far in the future. The boys had solved that problem with the ingenious drum system. A cam and push rod raised each plate in turn, lining it up in front of the eye clock's front lens, then reflecting the image via a pair of mirrors into the viewer. I had yet to find a cracked or broken fast plate. Each one must have been constructed of very high-quality glass. Every single one I had seen so far was framed with gilded copper strips to prevent cracking or chipping. A lot of money had gone into the eye clock. A lot of thought too.

Somehow, someone had broken the film speed barrier — the amount of light it takes to produce an image. One reason people in nineteenth-century photographic portraits look like they have a stick up their butts is that they just about do.

Subjects had their noggins strapped into iron frames resembling medieval torture devices to hold them still. With lengthy exposure time, even the slightest movement would result in blurring. And that's just for starters. After exposure, you would have to rush the exposed plate back to the darkroom — or dark wagon — for an elaborate process accomplished with dangerous chemicals.

All done in the absence of light. That's the reason there were no action photos from the era, or at least until now. Daguerreotypes were printed on polished copper plates faced with silver, so that was out. There was a wet Collodion process that came along in the late 1850s, but no one was making action movies with them. The process was still painstakingly elaborate and prone to failure at the slightest screw-up. Collodion used a glass plate medium, but like the daguerreotype, it was hampered by hellishly long exposure times. Still, the fast plate process was at least partially derived from the Collodion-based technology. I was hoping one of the other drums would provide a little more insight. I packed series #1 away and went to the next drum of plates.

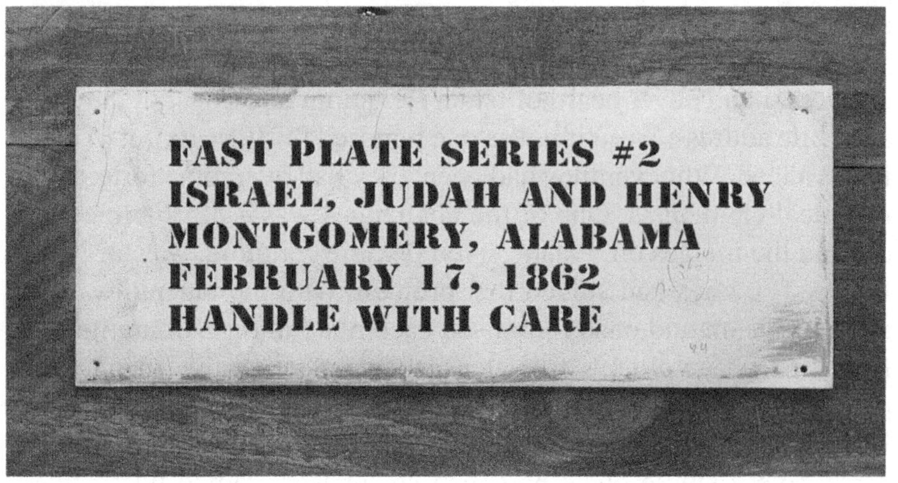

Now the camera was back in front of the State House, transformed into a new national Capitol building. Dressed to the nines, two men stood arm in arm at the bottom of the steps, smiling at the camera. Both were blessed with broad friendly faces so similar in features they must have been brothers or cousins. The one on the right was as unmistakable as Robert E. Lee. He was Judah P. Benjamin, the only really competent civilian leader in a hopelessly inept Confederate government. As secretary of state, he had come within an ace of convincing Britain to intervene on behalf of the South. He had only been thwarted by the South's inability to win a decisive victory on Northern soil. The longer the war dragged on, the more important he had become to the function of a faltering nation. He had done every job tasked to him with exceptional competence — secretary of state and secretary of war among them. He ended up doing everything but catch stray dogs and deliver the damn mail. In the final months of the war, he had wound up as Jeff Davis's right-hand man. The final testament to Benjamin's brilliance was that he had somehow escaped to England when everyone else in the upper levels of Rebel command had gotten pinched by the Feds.

Cantankerous old Jeff Davis might have ended up in chains, but not Judah Phillip Benjamin. He lived out the remainder of his life practicing law in London and made more money than Santa Claus. He died two decades after the war, well regarded by his adopted country.

I had always liked the wily old Hebrew. There are a good many ordinary pictures of him, and he always has the smile of a man who knows something you don't. That meant the other man in the images was almost certainly Israel Benjamin, the fast plate genius. The pair waved and smiled like they were at Daytona Beach on spring holiday. This timed out at exactly twenty seconds. Then the scene suddenly changed.

It was the first edit in the history of motion pictures. Now the subjects were the beaming Israel and a young Black boy about twelve- or thirteen-years old. The few other people of African extraction I had spotted in the first series had been bundled against the cold in little more than cast-off rags, but this young fellow was ready for a night on the town. He had an expansive brilliant smile, almost too big for his coal-black face. He looked at the camera with sharp, intelligent eyes. A good many early photos are of people who only have the dimmest idea of what is happening. This boy's eyes were needle-sharp, intelligent, and above all, knowing. Israel had one hand clapped on the young man's shoulder with unmistakably genuine affection, and his other hand pointed to the camera. The young man nodded, laughed, and waved at me across a one-hundred-thirty-year gap. It could only be Henry, Israel's son. A white adopting Black children back then was not unknown. The Davis family had done so, but it was hardly common.

I placed the drum back in its case, locked the barn door behind me, and went straight to the most indispensable resource a good forger has — his library. My old single-wide had more books and magazines about the Civil War crammed into it than the Museum of the Confederacy. It had started when I came down with tonsillitis and my folks bought me a subscription to *Civil War Times* as a get-well present. *CWT* had a pretty good run before going out of business in the mid-1970s, and I had every edition they had printed, all ninety-nine of them. You still see similar publications pop up every now and then, but they always go over ground that's been well traveled — Gettysburg and Shiloh (the death of Stonewall) — and events that will always sell to the casual reader. *CWT* was always meticulously researched and had a definite fondness for the obscure and forgotten details of the era. They had even published an index every few years, bless their hearts. On top of that, I had other, more dubious publications picked up in flea markets and swap meets. Don't know how I would have grifted without them.

Neptune's Warriors was a quarterly magazine published in the mid-1920s, dedicated to the transition from wind to steam. The Confederate Navy got a lot of play in *Neptune's Warrior*s because it had been obliged to be innovative to offset the overwhelming numerical superiority of the United States Navy. It was a good place to find information about the Rebel submarines, semi-submersibles, electrically triggered mines, and other extraordinary weapons. I had eleven copies recovered from the back seat of an old Packard sedan that had belonged to a retired naval officer. Besides these publications, I had enough books on the conflict and history in general packed into the single-wide to crush the blocks that held her off the ground. I've had more than a couple of dates over who invariably said the same thing at the sight of my library.

"You sure do have a whole lot of books."

This penetrating observation was always followed by another identical question.

"Have you actually read all of these?"

When I told them 'yes' I was almost always met with skepticism. No one could read that many books. Why in the hell would they? Well, I have read all of them, some more than once. There's a few of them I've ridden into the ground like a disposable war horse. I've read *Guns of August* through three printings. I read them until their spines broke, their covers fell off, and they began to shed leaves like a dying tree. And it wasn't because I was in the business of forging artifacts for a living. I just happen to like books. Besides, knowledge is power.

I not only read them, I'm pretty good at retaining the information, but I had never even had a hint about movies from the Civil War. I think I would have remembered that. I went through the *CWT* index noting every article on photography, but found nothing but the normal articles about Matthew Brady and his crew. There were quite a few words on Judah P. Benjamin but no radical new insights, no indication of a brother or cousin either. The big break came on the next-to-the-last page of *CWT*, April 1975, its last issue. By that time I was just flipping through copies at random, and I noticed an essay concerning the great Montgomery saloon riot. Seeing how there's nothing really unusual about a bar fight, I gave it a quick read to see what had made it so special.

It happened at an enchanting watering hole called the Cotton Bank Saloon on the hot, sticky night of July 4, 1860. The country was in an ugly mood, but in the heart of the cotton empire, it was absolutely militant. At the Cotton Bank, you had better be a hard-core secessionist or you wouldn't have much fun. Anyone in that place better have his head on straight or it would be adjusted for him. As you might have already guessed, the saloon was favored by the wealthy plantation owners, cotton exporters, and slave-trader types. The Cotton Bank had the distinction of being one of the most dangerous spots in Montgomery. When they didn't have an abolitionist to whip up on, they used each other for practice. On that sweltering summer night, an old customer came walking through the door.

It was August Day, a notorious slave trader who worked the South Tennessee/North Alabama circuit. Day was also well known as what today would be called a compulsive gambler. He went through cash as quickly as he earned it, and slavers made a lot of money. Always hard up for a quick payout, Day had brought in someone quite unusual for sale. Mr. Day had just acquired a young Negro boy who could be had for a bargain price. The denizens of the Cotton Bank shrugged their shoulders.

"So what? We've got a million more of them. The best ones cost half what you're asking for this skinny kid."

"Ahhhhh," said Mr. Day. "I bet you don't have any like this one."

Day stood the hapless young man on a soapbox kept for impromptu auctions as a curious crowd gathered. His first question was quite simple, but for me, it provided a big answer. "Henry, what is nine hundred thirty-two divided by eight?"

Henry replied without a trace of hesitation. "Yes sir, one hundred sixteen-and-a-half."

Day continued the show with no more regard for Henry than if he had been a trick pony. "Very good, Henry, can you tell me what seven thousand twenty-three is multiplied by eleven-and-a-half?"

"Yes sir, nine hundred twenty-seven thousand, thirty-six."

The clientele of Cotton Bank flatly refused to believe it; this had to be some sort of inconceivably vile trick. Everyone knew that it was necessary for some Negroes to do simple calculations, but they were simply incapable of higher math. Doubtless, the boy had memorized the answers to predetermined questions to give the illusion of this unnerving ability.

"That's where you're all wrong," replied August Day. "Go ahead and ask him to calculate a problem of your own choosing."

A half-drunk planter from South Georgia stepped forward. "Can you tell me what sixty-three thousand multiplied by one hundred thirty-two is?"

"Yes sir. Eight million three hundred sixteen thousand, even."

Another planter decided this was all too easy. "So you think you're smart? Tell me then. You're such a smart little Nigger, what's a prime number?"

"Yes sir, a prime number is any number that can be divided by two without a remaining fraction."

Now the Cotton Bank was filled with a hundred pairs of eyes, wide with shock, floating in an atmosphere of unease. Predictably, this goaded the crowd into more aggressive questioning.

Another man stepped forward. "You think you're some kind of smart, don't you, boy? All right then, can you tell us all how to find the area of a circle?"

"Yes sir, a person can find the area of a circle by the use of Pi."

The Cotton Bank rocked to the rafters with sarcastic laughter and more than a little relief.

"You mean to tell me that you can find the area of a circle with a piece of apple pie! Boy, you know better than to pull a white man's leg!"

Henry was unfazed and quite serious. "Oh, no sir, boss. The kind o' pie I'm talking about is... well... it's like a magic little number you see. The Pi I'm talking about is 3.14159. If you know how to attach this magic little number to a problem, it'll reveal the answer. There's all sorts of things you can do with it, sir."

August Day should have known better than to embarrass his

peers. Henry was probably old enough to know not to sound smarter than the boss, but in all fairness, the kid had been put up to it. I can see that's the exact moment when the two of them were in very real danger. In attempting a big score, August had committed the unpardonable sin of making a Negro appear more intelligent than a white. Henry had only tried to please the man who controlled his fate, and in doing so had slipped a noose around his own neck.

Since the beginning of slavery, masters had prized docile, compliant slaves who were just barely competent enough to perform assigned tasks. But not ones smarter than the masters. Those were worse than slaves who ran away. A slave on the run is nothing but an inconvenience. A slave smarter than the master presents a hazard to the whole sorry system. From the master's point of view, such a man or woman is worse than useless. Intelligence makes them too dangerous to even sell down the river. Doing that only passes the problem off to another peer. Sooner or later it'll come back to haunt the big mansion like Caesar's ghost. A truly intelligent slave has to be eliminated before he gives the other ones crazy ideas.

The crowd became very ugly in a big hurry. The planter who had been embarrassed by the lesson from Henry about the value of Pi must have been a little more confrontational than the others. He was the one that challenged August Day, demanding to know where he had acquired such an unnatural abomination. Day must have been drunk, crazy, stupid or a combination of all three, because he told them the truth.

"I acquired this young slave up in Lime County."

The issue was pressed.

"From whose plantation?"

"The old Pettus place."

I could feel the dread crackle through the Cotton Bank a century after the fact. The Pettus castle was a local legend. A legend that was at least partially true. It's easy to imagine the long menacing silence before the next question.

"August, you mean to tell me that this is one of the Niggers that murdered Theodore Pettus and his wife in their bed?!"

By now August must have tried to backpedal, but it was too late. The cat was out of the bag.

"Yes, but he's just a —"

August Day's answer was caught in his throat by an Arkansas toothpick. The Georgian had plunged the dagger into Day's esophagus to a chorus of cheers. It sounds like Day owed a lot of people in the crowd too much money for a little too long. The Cotton Bank jury was unanimous on the August Day verdict. Doubtless, he got what he deserved, but poor blameless Henry was with the wrong person in the wrong place at the worst time possible.

Helpless and terrified, Henry was dragged out the front door to the nearest sizable tree where a rope was already prepared. Henry was not allowed a final request, a blindfold, or a final preflight word with his maker. It was to be a summary execution of a ten-year-old child.

I got mad as hell just reading about it for a lot of reasons. Chief among them is that I've always hated a damn bully. Sometimes fate hates them too.

Just as the lynch mob was about to hoist Henry up into the next life, there was the distinctive bang of a firearm at close quarters. At that moment what had to be two of the Deep South's most courageous men shoved their way into the center of the action. One was a pistol-packing Judah P. Benjamin, a New Orleans lawyer come to town on some now-forgotten business. The other was his first cousin, Israel Benjamin, a highly regarded watchmaker and bon vivant from Mobile. The Benjamin boys were nobody's fools. Both men were packing modern, multiple-shot handguns.

The crowd jeered and blustered but nobody was up for a gunfight with a couple of heavily armed Hebrews. Israel freed Henry while Judah held the chicken-shit mob at bay with a revolver in each hand. The three of them retreated down the dark back alleys of nineteenth-century Montgomery as the mob took its frustration out on the local neighborhood. During the riot that followed, the Cotton Bank caught fire and burned to the ground, taking an entire city block along with it. There was no mention of anyone being charged with the cold-blooded murder of August Day.

The final sentence revealed something I already knew: young Henry was not only placed under the protection of the Benjamin boys, but he would be adopted as Israel's son.

The name of Theodore Pettus added another layer of authenticity to the story.

Now the Pettus place was a castle the way a freezer full of steaks is a cow, but the heaped-up ruins are still there. I should know; I've been there more times than I've been to court. It was on a different kind of field trip — squirrel hunting the swampy hardwood bottoms along the Tennessee River.

Despite being a sizable chunk of thick hardwood forest and unspoiled cypress swamps, the hunting was mediocre. Its main appeal was that the land wasn't really claimed or managed by anyone until the paper company took it over a few years back. Now it's just another pine tree plantation, but back then it was open country. Even then there was a gloomy darkness about the place that was hard to overlook.

Dad and I stopped once or twice at the ruins for a quick snack of crackers and cheese that we always ate in silence. It was a heap of massive, dressed stones imported from France, now covered in thick green moss and slowly sinking into the Alabama mud. On some of the blocks, one could still see big black streaks left by an intense fire.

It had once been a real medieval castle. Theodore Pettus had seen it during his honeymoon in Europe. He liked it so much that he bought it, had it shipped about a zillion miles to his family plantation, and reassembled. On the surface, it sounds rather charmingly romantic, just some little doo-dad for the new missus. He bought the entire structure, towers, crenellations, baily, curtain wall, drawbridge, and oh my, don't forget that charming dungeon, honey! There used to be a brochure at the county tourism office that told you all about it but ignored the most interesting part. That's local tourism boosters for you.

Whatever Theodore and Alice did in their new dungeon is anybody's guess, but it did lead to a major historical event the booster club would rather forget. The Lime County slave rebellion was one of the most bizarre and controversial events of its kind. On the night of October 31, 1859, a distant red glow was seen east of Tuscumbia on the south bank of the river. A wooden town surrounded by forest is always wary of fire, so several horsemen were dispatched to investigate. Shortly after dawn, both men were pounding back into town with horrifying news. A slave rebellion had flared up at the Pettus plantation.

Both conventional wisdom and popular opinion held that even the hint of a slave insurrection had to be instantly and ruthlessly suppressed, or it would spread like fire in a barn full of hay. On November 1, the Tuscumbia rifles were called to the colors and hundreds of white men were sworn in as temporary auxiliaries. Neighboring communities contributed their share of militia and volunteers, and within forty-eight hours an iron ring had been thrown around the Pettus plantation. They had done this sort of thing before.

The small army closed in on the plantation grounds to discover the last thing they expected. No one had run away. The castle was now only a burned-out hull containing the charred remains of Theodore and Mary Pettus. Questioned intensely, the slaves began to spin out a tale of torture, abuse and depravity that was shocking even by the somewhat loose standards of the times.

Slaves had been systematically raped and tortured to death. The militia was shown hidden graves, sweat boxes, and a long iron rail where slaves were chained in the open and starved for weeks at a time. The spark of rebellion had been provided when a young boy of eight or nine years had been chained to the rail. His crime was lifting books from the master's library. It could only have been Henry. The master announced that the child's bones would remain there forever as an example of what happened to thieves at the Pettus plantation. The child's horrified mother had attempted to free the boy, but the poor woman had been shot dead by the missus for her trouble. That had been the last straw.

Whatever the militia and sheriff found, what followed is remarkable. There were no show hangings of the ringleaders to illustrate the perils of rebellion. Under militia supervision, the slaves were set to work tearing down the burnt-out remains of the castle. The contents of the dungeon were cast into the roiling waters of the Tennessee River. The burial sites of Theodore and Mary Pettus are unknown, but it's a better-than-even bet they sleep with the snapping turtles. The surviving slaves were allowed to give their kin decent Christian burials and were subsequently sold off to defray the cost of fielding the little army. Then the whole thing was swept under the rug and allowed to fade from memory.

I would have put the whole tale in a category including haunted bridges, but when I was still in high school, mussel divers found a large iron object while feeling their way through the silt. The salvage team expected an old safe or cannon. They brought up a corroded iron maiden typically found in fourteenth-century Europe. Further searching brought up cruel tongs designed only to tear flesh, and an iron boot used to crush the toes and feet of its unfortunate wearer. The ruins of the castle were less than a mile away.

You had to really admire this kid Henry. Not only was he a genius, but also he had the knack of survival. August Day had probably picked him up for next to nothing when the Pettus place was liquidated. Dollar signs must have popped up in the creepy old slaver's eyes when he discovered Henry's talent, but only disappointment followed. Nobody wanted Henry any more than a dose of the clap. He may have been completely innocent of wrongdoing but he had been central to the outbreak of a rebellion, hardly a strong selling point. Besides, the kid was unnaturally smart; he would be nothing but trouble down the line. In a delectable twist of fate, Day had found himself chained to a fifty-five-pound Black white elephant. It had gotten so bad he had gone to the Cotton Bank as a last resort.

The *CWT* went into a manila envelope, pretty thin stuff to base provenance on, but it made a fair starting point. If I was ever going to unload it for what it was worth, I'd have to build an ironclad case concerning its authenticity. I had plenty of confidence in my research ability, but proving that I owned the fast plates might be a little tougher. I couldn't just go walking in the back door of the Smithsonian peddling drums of fast plates like vacuum cleaners. There would be all sorts of awkward questions — like, where I found them and wasn't it true I had been convicted of fraud and trespassing. It was time to look at another drum. I walked outside and was mildly shocked that it was already dark. I glanced at my watch — 10:30 — time for the next drum of fast plates.

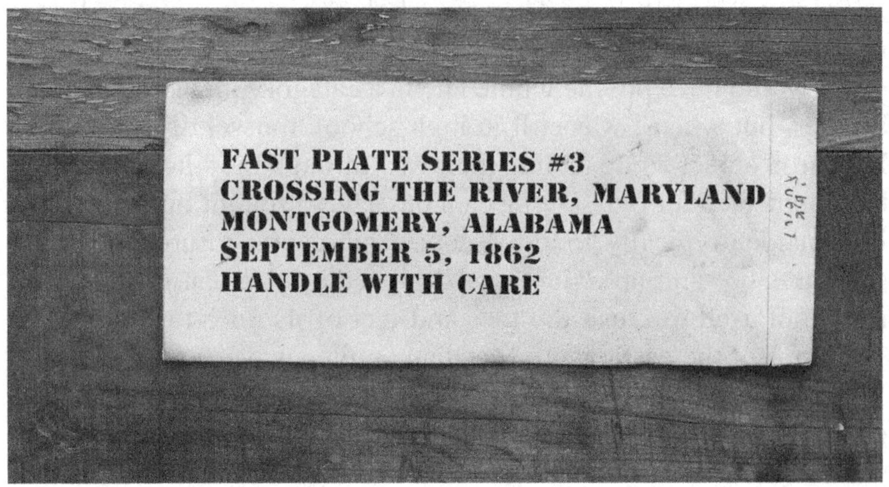

My heart sank a little when I pulled back the crumbling silk and caught the gleam of broken glass in the bottom of the case. I carefully lifted out the heavy drum and cussed a blue streak as shards of glass fell away like broken Christmas ornaments. I methodically pulled every single plate and repaired what I could. Twelve plates were beyond salvation, but with patience and Super Glue, I managed to repair the rest of the series. I eased the drum into the eye clock as gently as possible, adjusted the light, and turned the crank. The image was far grainier than the others, with a two-second gap halfway through the loop, but it was good enough.

The camera was looking across a broad shallow river. A line of gaunt, hard-looking men with cloths hanging from the bayonets of sloped muskets was trudging single file through the water, their bare butts shining like the harvest moon. Suddenly they stopped and cut loose with soundless cheers, waving their ragged hats in the air. Then a team of four harnessed horses silently splashed by, towing one of the South's most prized and exotic weapons. It was the unmistakable profile of a four-inch Whitworth gun. I stopped the drum and studied the long steel tube and bulky breech. There was no doubt; no other weapon in the world had the same lines as an English Whitworth.

The Rebels had managed to snatch up a few of them on credit early in the war before the Federal blockade really began to bite. The English-made Whitworths were state-of-the-art artillery in 1862.

Rapid-firing breech-loaders, they had a strange hexagonal bore and fired solid steel bolts accurately out to a range of nearly four miles.

They were cranky and temperamental, but crewed by the right men, they were as deadly as a modern sniper rifle shooting a twelve-pound bullet. I turned the crank — another Whitworth came splashing by followed by an ammunition caisson as the waving infantry silently cheered and hurrahed. In the last five seconds of the drum, a lone horseman brought up the rear as the half-naked infantry shouted even louder. I felt like shouting too. I knew who the horseman was.

It was Lee's gallant young warrior, the legendary John Pelham. The West Point dropout had caught Stuart's eye and been placed in charge of a small, highly mobile detachment of horse guns equipped with the exotic Whitworths. Anyone who had third-grade Alabama history in the mid-1960s learned what an astute choice J.E.B. Stuart had made. Barely old enough to vote, Pelham had played the deadly breech-loaders like a virtuoso violinist plays a Stradivarius. At Fredericksburg, he had come right into the open under a hundred enemy guns and slaughtered Yankee infantry like he was mowing the lawn. He and his surviving gunners galloped to safety only after expending all of their ammunition. It had been my favorite chapter in *Knowing Alabama*; it was like seeing an old friend, an old friend who was headed for a bad ending.

I wanted to warn him, to reach down into the eye clock, grab his magnificent charger by the bridle, and talk some sense into the boy. A sudden depression washed over me like a flood of blue mud. Even if I had been there, even if I could have seen into the future and Pelham had believed me, it would have changed nothing. He would have laughed me off with the certainty of indestructible youth, and I would have been strapped to a wagon wheel and flogged for harassing an officer. He had an unbreakable appointment with destiny and there wasn't shit anyone could do about it, then or now. On March 16, 1863, against express orders from both Stuart and Lee, he had gone freelancing and got involved in a minor skirmish he had no business in. His reward had been a chunk of shrapnel through his beautiful head. Lee and countless other hardened warriors had wept at the news of his death. Now it was my turn.

I have always been a loner, but happy with my own company. I've rarely felt alone. To the contrary, I had always gloried in the lack of attachments. My tears at the sight of John Pelham, healthy and full of life, were completely unexpected. I sat in the barn for a long time trying to regain my composure, embarrassed at myself and for myself, struggling to understand how the fast plates had brought me from the euphoria of discovery to near-suicidal depression. It's not like I had known any of the old Rebels or was even a distant relative to the famous ones. Even if I had been there, I would have had few political views in common with them; indeed, I probably would have been branded as a Yankee sympathizer, although I have no love for the North's actions during the war. Even a dog has the right to defend its home.

I forget if it was Grant or Sherman who said, 'Never was so much blood, toil, and suffering lavished on such a worthless cause as Southern independence.' As much dislike as I have for both men and their criminal methods, I agree wholeheartedly with their assessment. What we inherited as a unified nation is far superior to the deformed monstrosity that was strangled in its cradle. The Confederate States of America would have been a pariah nation, mired in an archaic philosophy that holds one man's life superior to another's simply because of who his parents were. Surrounded by enemies and spurned by a progressing world, we would have violently lashed out at the mere hint of a threat when we weren't squabbling among ourselves. Lee had complained that all the Confederate Congress was good for was to eat parched peanuts and spit chewing tobacco. I doubt if their performance would have improved with time. Davis was bullheaded in the extreme and refused to face the reality of failure even after the door to Richmond was kicked in and Honest Abe was practically walking up the stairs.

The last few plates of the series were jumpy and a little blurred from water damage, but Pelham was still unbelievably handsome and popular with even the most hapless web-footed Rebel grunts. I studied the last plate in the series through the eye clock; Pellham was looking directly at the camera with a wide bright smile lighting up his face. I wondered what he saw and thought to myself: *was he wondering what this civilian and young Negro boy were about?*

Were they grinding coffee, ginning cotton, or what?

I have no idea what the original fast plate camera looked like, but if anything, in that situation and time, the first guess would be some sort of newfangled weapon. If he had any anxiety about being the target of this bizarre machine, he didn't show it. Pelham was plunged up out of the water without the slightest trace of hesitation and was gone. Like every soul ever born to woman, he had a date with destiny, but in his case he seemed perfectly content with his lot.

I stopped my stopwatch: fast plate run time, twenty-eight seconds.

"Good luck, Johnny."

My gasp almost echoed in the empty barn. I understood why I had become so overwhelmed by the sight of Pelham. He was my friend, as good a friend as I've ever had in this life, and I was loath to see him come to harm. The realization hit me like a bale of hay dropped from the loft. I loved them all, even the unlovable ones. I loved them despite their idiot politics and ridiculous goals. I loved them because I was like them, desperately trying to pound the round peg of the world into the square hole of desired reality. Only they were better than me. They had been willing, eager even, to go to the mat, to face impossible odds, suffer, starve, to kill or be killed, trying to prove their point.

Me? I was just a half-assed con man who had snipped off bits of their glory and courage the way people used to shave gold coins on the sly. For the first time in my life, I was truly ashamed to even be alive. I began to fear for the fast plates. A lot of people wouldn't like them, and not because they were possibly fraudulent. Motion made men like Davis and Pelham just as human as anyone alive today. Outside the South, the war has been almost forgotten by the United States, while deep in Louisiana and Alabama, the memories still refuse to just die. I've had more than one Northerner shake his head in disbelief over our persistence of memory. I had always put that view down to the fact that with one major exception, all fighting had been on Southern soil and total war had been waged against the civilian population. Now I could see it ran a lot deeper than that. Defeat hadn't just caused us to doubt the cause; defeat made us question our fitness to exist.

I decided then and there that the United States government would never own the fast plates. I would smash them with a hammer first. They would never be displayed in the Smithsonian or the National Archives like a stuffed bear killed by Teddy Roosevelt. I hadn't decided what to do with them, but that was all right. I had plenty of time to sort that out. I was dog-tired. I had no idea of what time it was or even what day it was, but I was way too wired up for sleep! I would watch the final two drums, somehow already knowing they would complete the unfolding story of my new pals, Israel and Henry. Then I would know what to do.

Men were trudging past the camera four abreast along a narrow dark road with new-looking rifles sloped over their shoulders. Some had shoes or short boots, but more were barefoot. One lean man slogged past close enough to reach out and touch the lens, giving me my most detailed view so far. I stopped the drum to give him a closer examination. He wore dark pants and a short pale jacket with frayed sleeves and blown-out elbows. He wasn't carrying much equipment. A wooden canteen bounced on one hip, presumably balanced with a cartridge box on the other. On his back was a small leather pack with what looked like someone's Persian carpet tightly rolled and strapped to the top. He was hatless and young. Without the scraggly whiskers and dirt, he would have looked even younger. A new Enfield Pattern rifle was sloped across his bony shoulder. In the background beyond the road, a few horses were being held by enlisted types who watched other men take down a medium-sized tent as others loaded something into a wagon. Then, at twelve seconds there was another abrupt edit.

An older man with a full white beard removed a straw hat and peered intently into the lens. Even if he wasn't wearing the hot-looking coat with stars on the collar, he was instantly recognizable. The face on the plate was the venerated and dreaded Robert Edward Lee, Marse Robert himself. I stopped the eye clock, stood up, and took a deep breath. Just finding a previously unknown Collodion plate of Lee would have caused a major sensation, but I would never have dared to even fantasize a fast plate sequence of the man. Without him the plates had been worth a wheelbarrow full of money; with him they were now virtually priceless. I rubbed my eyes, moved the backlight a little closer, and pressed my brow to the viewing window while trying to ignore my pounding heart. Was I seeing only what I subconsciously wished for?

It might not be him; there were thousands of older men serving under the Rebel colors. It might well be a regimental surgeon or some other senior officer. There's one famous picture of Lee and the miserably unappreciated Joe Johnson taken a few years after the war. Wearing dark civilian clothing and facing each other over a small table, the two bearded men could have passed as twins who were starting to get on in years. Trying to avoid foregone conclusions, I took a closer look at the old man. He was darkly tanned with thin dark lines of the grueling march ground into his face. There was a motion behind him as the lines of men parted to reveal a ragged groom walking a pale, spotted horse across the road. It was the most renowned war horse since Bucephalas. It was Traveller, and his master was Lee.

At seventeen seconds the old man indulged himself in an impish grin, glanced to one side, and with the wave of a gloved hand, motioned someone to come closer. Another face crowded into the frame. The man was younger, mid-thirties or so. His face was covered with thick untamed whiskers under a slumping old forage cap that nearly covered the pale eyes of a cold-blooded killer. Lee pointed at me through the camera. The bearded man scowled with disapproval, shook his shaggy head and spoke.

The words were easy to lip-read. "Looks like the devil's work to me."

Lee laughed and shook his head knowingly; the shaggy man lifted a small object to his mouth. I stopped the drum and examined what he was eating; it appeared to be a small lemon. He was a man who used to frighten the Yankees like Hannibal terrified the Romans. His eccentricities were legendary, his faith was in a benevolent God without limits, and some historians have even questioned his mental stability. Not something I would have recommended doing to his face. This was the South's most redoubtable warrior of all. The man Lee had called into the frame was Lieutenant General Thomas Jackson, known to the ages as Stonewall. Fast plate run time: thirty seconds.

By anyone's measure, Tom Jackson was an odd duck, albeit a dangerous one. He was loath to fight on a Sunday and would only do so when cornered. His students at the Virginia Military Academy had called the aloof professor of artillery, "Tom Fool." Like many professional soldiers, it's almost certain he was partially deaf, and this probably contributed to his reputation as a mildly absent-minded professor. He had once been involved in a minor scandal for teaching Blacks the basics of reading, but had refused to back down, striking back at his foes in pointed Jacksonian style. He used a surprising and almost outlandish flanking maneuver.

Salvation came only through the Holy Gospel and only the literate could read the Bible; therefore, he was obligated as a Christian to teach anyone willing how to read. His critics had enough intelligence not to press the issue. One of his favorite treats was sucking a lemon the way normal people might enjoy a good sweet orange. In battle he was cool as Jack Frost, absolutely without fear, and could frequently be seen on horseback, his right hand raised in prayer as mini balls zipped through the air like a rain of lead hailstones. He passed out religious tracts in camp like a Jehovah's Witness, and black pepper made his legs hurt. A severe disciplinarian, his troops feared him almost as much as the enemy, but they loved him too. When Jackson died after a friendly fire incident, the hopes of Southern independence died with him. The brilliant Lee carried on after Thomas Jackson was gone, but the old indomitable spirit was never quite the same.

I would never be the same either. I could name my price if I could find the right buyer, but who? If I hadn't screwed myself with the sword thing, I would still be running a tidy little business, but now my name was mud from Vicksburg to Stuttgart. Well, there are always options, even if they're not readily apparent. One of my problems has been that I always get wound up over shit way too easily. All I had to do was get a grip on myself and the solution would appear like green in the spring. My Celtic monster, Peter Flynn, sent the message that if he ever caught wind of me being back up to my old tricks, he would do the world a big fat favor. I might not be the truest arrow in the quiver but I'm also not a complete idiot. I knew exactly what he meant, and he would be all too happy to give the order. The son of a bitch was nearly ten years younger than me, so just waiting till he kicked the bucket first was out. There was always the outside chance that he would get whacked or busted, but the guy had more lives than Buddha's house cat. A good many high-powered politicians loved his pouch-sucking money like baby kangaroos suck milk.

Suppose I could sell them as individual plates? Nope, that would be futile. At first I might slip by, but it wouldn't be long till a couple of collectors made a connection. They were the kind of stupid fucks that would rat to the big boys on the chance they could get in on the kill. Expert witnesses aren't cheap. There was a time when I might have taken the chance, just moved faster than word could catch up, and when I had enough money, vanish. The way things were now, that would be virtually impossible. With two strikes already against me, there was a real possibility that I could end up doing hard time.

I looked at Lee and Jackson again and again. I watched them until I felt like I was standing behind the fast plate camera, a few golden seconds of intimate interaction with the most feared team of warriors in Western history. I was their pal and confidant and I told them things no man has a right to know. They dismissed my concerns with a genteel disdain and gave me a little advice of their own. They say free advice is worth exactly what you pay for it. They might be right a lot of the time, but not all the time.

I began to formulate an audacious flanking maneuver of my own. It was bold, dangerous, and more than a little crazy, but it beat washing dishes at Leo's truck stop all to hell. The hard part would be ginning up the nerve to attempt it. If I screwed up, it was curtains for old Jim Broadfoot.

Marse Robert and Stonewall approved. I was so exhausted that my body felt like it was stuffed with cotton, but there was one more thing to do before I hit the sleeping bag — watch the final drum of plates. I had noticed this crate had been a little lighter than the others. After removing the top and peeling back the packing, I saw why. A good third of the plates was missing. There couldn't be more than twenty seconds running time here. I settled the drum into the gears of the eye clock, locked down the top, and gently turned the crank.

Swirling clouds of smoke mixed with smeared blots of man-shaped shadows. A jumbled line of lean, ragged men hunkered down for cover in what looked like a shallow rock quarry, firing at unseen targets hidden behind gritty fog. Behind them, soldiers reloaded Enfield rifle-muskets, capped them, and passed them to the front with unbelievable speed. The reloaders had dispensed with ramrods altogether, just pouring in the powder and ball, then slamming the butts of the weapons on the hard ground to ram home the charge. It was the fastest way known to seat a round in the archaic muzzleloaders but damned hard on the wooden furniture.

There were several shapes on the ground I had assumed were just blankets and rucksacks shucked by the troops, but then one of them began to crawl away with his last ounce of life. There were more rifles than shooters. Whoever these guys were, they were taking one hell of a pounding.

I knew in the first five seconds these boys were in an awkward spot. No officer would willingly allow this brutal abuse of weapons unless they had their backs to the wall. I turned the crank with a deliberate slowness, reducing the motion to little more than flip-book speed. A tall wiry officer came into the middle ground, waving his slender sword and banging away with a revolver.

The enemy was close enough to hit with a slingshot. As the officer bullied and fired, I noticed a man with a dangling arm sitting on the ground desperately searching through black leather ammo pouches with his one good hand, a sure sign they were running out of gas, and fast. Another few minutes and they would be throwing rocks at the Yanks like Jackson's foot calvary at the Battle of Second Manassas. Then suddenly, an abrupt gap opened in the smoke.

A few hundred yards away down a steep slope you could plainly see a triple-arched stone bridge with a dark mass surging across, several stands of colors being carried before and among them, and officers out front urging the men forward over their dead and dying friends. Geysers of white water spurted up out of the creek, chunks of stone flew off the bridge, and limp bodies tumbled into the water below. The head of the column hesitated, then surged forward with a vengeance. Given the date on the box, the sturdy stone bridge, the position of the defenders, and the numbers of the attackers, it could only be one thing. It was the Battle of Antietam, or Sharpsburg if you prefer, and after the fight, that stone span would always be known as Burnside Bridge. The ridge was being held by Robert Toombs' decimated Georgia Brigade, now down to barely enough warm bodies to fill out a couple of contemporary platoons.

For some reason never satisfactorily explained, General Ambrose Burnside had ordered a frontal attack right into the teeth of the Georgians when there were several uncontested crossings less than a mile upstream. He might have thought the Rebels on the ridge had been so badly mauled that he had the numbers to shove them out of the way. He thought wrong. The smoke closed in, and I stopped the eye clock as I hacked my stopwatch, fifteen seconds in. There couldn't be more than another five or six seconds. My eyelids were thin sheets of lead. I rubbed my hand across my face and felt heavy stubble. Grunting with effort, I grasped the handle and turned the final seconds.

The unknown officer turned and shouted at his boys. I could lip-read a single word on his silent lips: "Courage!" Then he spun around like someone had clocked him upside the head with a Louisville slugger, and flopped motionless to the ground. A sudden shape dashed into the frame. He was well fed but his clothing was a few sizes too large. His coat was gone. He wore dark pants, a torn white shirt with the sleeves rolled up and a nice silk vest spattered with dark spots. His whiskers were now as long as an old-world rabbi's but they couldn't hide the broad honest face. The gallant Israel Benjamin scooped up the fallen man with a single powerful motion, fueled by sheer adrenaline, and began to carry the stricken officer away from the embankment. Israel's right leg billowed up like an overinflated toy balloon and the two of them collapsed in a thrashing heap. The sequence had run its course. I hacked the stopwatch and looked at the hands. Fast plate run time: twenty-one seconds.

I threw the watch against the wall of the barn where it burst into a hundred flying springs and gears. Judah and Henry had recorded the first live combat footage in history. I could see it all in my mind's eye. They had set the fast plate camera on the ridge above Antietam Creek where they could record in relative safety. Israel and Henry had probably been advised by Toombs that this was a fairly well protected position. Israel had directed while Henry had assumed the role of cameraman. Protected by the ferocious Georgia sharpshooters who held the high ground, they probably felt reasonably secure. Only a homicidal madman who hated his own troops would have attempted a cattle stampede across the narrow span. The nameless officer must have been a close friend; Israel had rushed to his aid and been hit himself. Henry had abandoned the camera and had hurried to help his father.

What happened to Israel and Henry after that was now an agonizing mystery. Burnside's men had eventually clawed their way across and up the ridge to drive off the Georgia Brigade's survivors, but it wrecked the units involved. Few of Toombs' men had escaped. Israel had obviously been severely wounded. As improbable as it seems, they must have gotten away in the nick of time. The very existence of the last drum of plates proved that. In a situation like this, the camera would have drawn storms of enemy fire. It was big and weird looking; it might have even been mounted on wheels and been trundled about like a small artillery piece. The Rebels had already developed a well-earned reputation for infernal machines, so the Yanks would have assumed the worst concerning its purpose.

The retreat from Maryland had been almost as horrific as the fighting. Loaded down with thousands of wounded men bouncing along the macadam roads in springless wagons, the retreat had degenerated into a march through hell. They wouldn't have been difficult to track. The mauled army had left a trail of blood like some great wounded beast. The army of Northern Virginia retained its cohesion only because of the charisma of its leaders and the unbreakable determination of the survivors to escape. If the timid McClellan had had more nerve, he could have mopped up what remained of the Confederacy's premier field army in a couple of days. McClellan had an entire army corps that hadn't fired off a single shot on that terrible day, but he had learned to be wary of Lee and Jackson the hard way. The army of Northern Virginia escaped and survived to fight another day. The egotistical and timid McClellan was sacked shortly thereafter.

Had Israel survived? It's hard to believe that Henry would have abandoned him. Henry wouldn't have been harmed if the Yanks had caught him, but they wouldn't have done him any favors either. Henry would have ended up like thousands of other Black refugees: doing laundry and digging ditches for Uncle Sam. No, they had escaped along with Lee's shattered army.

I staggered to my sleeping bag in the old cow stall and slept the sleep of the dead. It's not unusual at all for the dead to visit me in my dreams. A Jungian psychologist would dismiss the visits as only symbolic of the losses and insecurity of life, but I know better. The deceased may visit me but they rarely speak. When they do, I have learned to listen hard and well. Sometimes the dead reveal the future, but the information seems so meaningless and jumbled that Sitting Bull would be hard-pressed to provide the proper interpretation. It's all just a bucket of surreal garbage until the event actually comes to pass. That night as I slept in the old barn stall, something new happened: a visit from someone I knew of but had never known.

In my dream, there was a knock on my trailer's thin plastic and aluminum door. I struggled to rise off the couch, fighting against the unseen bonds that held me down as the pounding grew louder and more aggressive. I could hear a muffled, unfamiliar voice calling my name as I tumbled off the couch and began to crawl on all fours through empty beer cans and stacks of books that kept toppling over to strike me on the back and head. The knocking grew so violent that the flimsy door threatened to jump from its hinges. I could see a bright ethereal light streaming through the space between the door and frame. Again, an unfamiliar voice shouted at me.

"Git up! Git up and get moving, you damned little scoundrel!"

I reached up for the doorknob. My fingers slipped and fumbled with the shoddy plastic. I found my voice and called beyond the door. "Israel? Israel? Henry? Ya'll quit kicking my door! I'm comin' as fast as I can. Wait. Wait."

"I ain't got time to wait! I move fast and you better move fast too!"

"Israel? No need to be nasty, friend, I'm almost there. You woke me up."

"You damn fool, I ain't Israel and I sure as hell ain't that boy of his! Open this door this instant!"

My voice sounded weak and far off down a dusty canyon. "Who... who is it? You got a warrant?"

"It is Ambrose Powell Hill and I don't require a damned warrant! Now open this door before I kick it in!"

Finally, I crawled to my feet and pulled myself upright. I pressed one eye to the peephole, but all I could see was a blinding golden light. "A.P. Hill? Hang on General Hill. Hang on. I've almost got it."

The door finally swung open and there was A.P. Hill, sunken cheeks, flowing waterfall of whiskers, red shirt and all. I slopped out a clumsy salute as Hill looked me up and down with sharp critical eyes. A golden aura surrounded his gaunt body, and he looked impatient. I squinted into the land behind him. It was the bright dreamlike landscape of a Renaissance painting. Hill stepped past the threshold and gave my quarters a disapproving look.

"Hello General Hill, are you feeling well?"

This seemed to please him immensely, and he indulged himself in an approving smile. "Why thank you for your concern, yes, I've never felt better. My stomach doesn't bother me a lick anymore. I appreciate your concern, Jimmy, but I am here to issue orders!"

Jimmy? No one had ever called me Jimmy except my long-departed mother. I nodded enthusiastically. He must have met her beyond the wall that separates us all from the land of eternal rest. I felt slightly cheated. Why couldn't it have been her or even Daddy? I had so much to apologize for. A bold thought hit me; this might be my chance to get something right for a change.

"Yes sir, what would you have of me?"

"I would have you move fast, that's what! We's all tired to death of watching you back down here moving like a terrapin on a cold day. You know that flanking march you been thinking about? Quit thinking about it and do it! If you strike now, all will be well."

"You mean the way you came up from Harper's Ferry? You saved Lee's army that day, you know?"

"I saved your friends Israel and Henry too. Now it's time to save you. Now march and march hard!"

I leaned against the frame. The land beyond looked so beautiful and peaceful and I wanted to step into it and away from here. "I'm ashamed to admit this, sir, but I'm scared shitless."

Hill shrugged his bony shoulders. "Of course you are, Jimmy. If you weren't, there would be something wrong with you, but there comes a time when you just have to cut cards with the devil. Goodbye, Jimmy. Don't fret, we'll meet again."

Hill began to shrink like Styrofoam in gasoline as the golden light began to fade. The wonderful valley of bliss was rapidly dissolving.

"No wait! Take me with you!"

Hill shook his shaggy face, placed a broad-brimmed hat on his head, and began to close the door behind him.

"In your own time, Jimmy, in your own time. March hard, Mr. Broadfoot, march till your feet are raw. You march till you drop and all will be well."

Hill slammed the door and the light faded.

Now awake, I was on my back looking up at the old loft. Dust motes danced in thin beams of sunlight that slanted between cracks in the wall. I got to my feet and looked around at the cases of tropical hardwood and the silent eye clock. I felt like I had been beaten with a club and tossed onto the side of a country road the night before. A hot shower and a cup of coffee brought me back to the living. I pondered all five drums and made my selection carefully. It had to be enough to pique Mr. Flynn's interest, but not so outlandish that it would only piss him off.

I chose one of five plates that wouldn't completely preclude the possibility that the plates were fake, but my choice would go a good ways in proving the veracity of what I had to offer — Jeff Davis taking the oath of office, Judah and Israel, Johnny Pelham looking right at the camera, Lee playfully teasing Tom Jackson, and finally, the nameless officer holding the ridge. Breaking out the jigsaw, I cut thin frames for each plate from scraps of plywood, sandwiching the delicate images between them. On top of that, I taped the cleanest cardboard I could find and wrapped the assembled packages in masking tape. I had just enough bubble pack to wrap each precious plate and packed the entire collection in a cardboard box that my last decent pair of boots had come in.

I had enough money for shipping, but it was all in Morgan dollars and wedding bands. I took four of the best coins down to Lawrence Pistol and Pawn where nobody ever asked me any uncomfortable questions, but the tradeoff was making deals just short of being cheated at three-card monte. I got seventy-five dollars for five extra-fine Morgans. Normally, after being offered such an insulting sum, I would have stomped out in a huff, but you got to spend money to make money.

I rushed home to find the barn door still locked. Ye gods how I hated to turn my back on the fast plates! I was seeing deputies and desperado cocaine addicts behind every bush and stop sign. Traffic was still tearing up and down the road like normal, both drivers and passengers ignorant of the fortune that was in the old barn behind the diapered single-wide.

I got to the post office fifteen minutes before they closed the window and put the package in for next-day air, insured for an eyebrow-raising five grand. The flanking march was underway. I had just enough money left for a tank of gas and a few sacks of groceries, including the first good steak I had bought in recent memory. Back home I moved everything into the bedroom of the trailer, took a long hot shower and ate the best meal of my life. It's amazing what a steady diet of store-brand grits and cheap country ham will do for the appetite. I spent the rest of the evening improvising a fighting position in the trailer with thick walls of history books and magazines. Then I oiled, loaded, and prepositioned every gun I still owned. I was ready. Nothing to do now but rest and wait.

It's said that June 6, 1944, was the longest day in history. That may be true, but the day after I shipped the package ran a near second place. I knew I still had from thirty-six to forty-eight hours before the balloon went up, and that's a long time for a situation like this to prey on your mind. I washed the dishes, took out the garbage, and even vacuumed around a little. Parking the Mustang out back, I loaded her up with a packed suitcase, the remaining coins and jewelry, and slipped a loaded .22 pistol into the glove compartment. I purposely avoided taking any more looks through the eye clock or even at the individual fast plates. I had decided I would never look at the plates again. In case things went sour when I made contact with the enemy, I took precautions so no one would ever see them again. I had a gallon of gas and a railroad flare ready for use. The fast plates would leave here my way, or they would never leave at all. I had my second consecutive night of sound, dreamless sleep.

I was up and ready well before dawn. The package had probably arrived and been opened late in the day at his main real estate office in Boston. Unless it got tossed into a pile of junk mail or had been lost in transit, the wheels of fate were already turning. I spent the day double- and triple-checking every weapon, improving the firing loops in my walls of books, and flipping through back issues of *Civil War Times*. I hadn't had a phone since my little business went belly up. If he wanted to talk to me or anything else, he would have to come to me.

I had almost given up for the day when a pair of anonymous cars pulled into my driveway just after supper. They were airport rental jobs, so he had sent out a team almost immediately. I checked my .38 as I watched them through the window. It was the man himself escorted by three of his goons, big thick Irish types with flattened noses and an air of menace floating around them like a cloud of red-headed flies around a rotting catfish.

Peter Flynn walked to the door alone while two of his boys hung back, and a third eased around behind the trailer. He pounded on the door like Hill had done in my dream, but this time I was awake and ready. He wasn't a big man, but those cold blue eyes and reputation more than made up for his lack of size. Flynn was the intense kind of man who commanded respect even if you didn't know what he was about. I patted the hard lump of steel in my back pocket, said my prayers, and opened the door.

"Good evening, Mr. Flynn, it's nice to see you. How have you been?"

Flynn didn't smile. "That's just like one of you treasonous Johnny Rebs, always polite even after you've had a well-deserved thrashing. You're typical of your people, Broadfoot, shortchanged by God on good sense, but you got balls. I'll say that for you."

I shrugged and managed a wan smile; surely he could hear my heart beating. "I've always felt bad about that little misunderstanding between us, Mr. Flynn. Would you and your associates care for a cup of tea and some cookies?"

"I didn't drop my business and fly down to this Godforsaken place for a cup of fuckin' tea, boyo. You try any cute bullshit and it'll take you a long time to die. Show me what you got."

"Of course, Mr. Flynn, please come in."

Flynn stepped inside and looked around my single-wide. "Jesus and Mother Mary have mercy. This makes the old home in Cork look like Buckingham Palace." He stopped and looked hard at the wall of books, then grudged me an appreciative grin. "I've known people to hide behind books, Jim, but never seen anyone build a fortress from them. Expecting trouble, boyo?"

"Better safe than sorry, Mr. Flynn. Let me introduce you to the fast plates. It involves a previously unknown Collodion process invented by a man named Israel Benjamin and his son Henry around the year 1860. I discovered them only a few days ago."

There was an immediate change in Flynn's demeanor. The more I talked the more confident I became. It was like the old days but only better. This was an honest one-in-a-million find. An hour later his men had the eye clock and fast plates loaded up in the rental cars and were pulling out onto the road, headed north at a high rate of speed. Ten grand doesn't seem like much for what Flynn walked away with and it's not, but I did enjoy watching them pool all the cash they had with them. Plus there was the added bonus of no shootout followed by a conflagration that consumed us all, along with the first movies ever made. My flanking march had been a success; the fast plates were no longer slung around my neck like a glass albatross. There is no taste like the taste of victory.

I felt aimlessly lost for a few days. I tried to fill in the hours by catching up on bills and putting just enough in the bank to get me out of the red without looking like I had knocked over a grocery store. It was the Mustang that brought me back around. After changing the plugs and oil, I washed and waxed my sweet baby and took her out for a new pair of shoes. My drive home was my victory parade and the exquisite roar of the 289 was my brass band. I laughed and sang forgotten old songs. Tiger paws didn't look this good on a real tiger. I was dreaming of my cut-rate European vacation when I pulled into my driveway, but the sight of a strange yellow van parked in front of my single-wide gave me a serious anxiety attack. Unlocking the glove compartment I retrieved the .22 just as a middle-aged woman came walking from behind my trailer.

She saw me and waved, then began to walk toward the car with a box under one arm and a clipboard in her other hand. I relaxed a little, but not much. I put the pistol on the passenger seat and covered it with an old towel. Hit men come in all shapes, sizes and sexes. I've never shot at a girl, but there's a first time for everything. I sat in the car watching the woods for movement but saw nothing but a pair of redbirds going about their normal avian business. If she was here to do me, she was here to do me alone.

"Are you Mr. James Broadfoot?"

I nodded and watched for a wrong move. She smiled hopefully and came closer. "I have a package for you from Yankee Patriot Real Estate in Boston, Massachusetts. I would have left it on your stoop, but I have to have a signature."

I watched her carefully. A single second of misplaced trust and it could be lights out forever.

"Mister Broadfoot, are you all right?"

She wasn't terribly good looking and didn't seem inclined toward fitness or even intimidating bulk. I slowly got out of the car, wary of the entire world.

She tilted her head curiously and then nodded as she understood. "I'm from Mason Overnight Delivery. I'm sorry, do you have an ID?"

"So, I've seen your trucks here and there. Don't they have one for you?"

"Mine's in the shop and this is a rental. Look, you want this or not? I've got a lot of deliveries to make."

I set the package on my workbench and studied it for a solid hour. Finally deciding that if he had wanted to work me harm, he would have done it days ago. I began to open the package with a single-edged razor blade. I cut the tape and lifted the cardboard flaps like I was lifting an anti-personnel mine. No bright flash of eternity — just an envelope on top of a box full of Styrofoam peanuts. I sliced open the paper and pulled out a Hallmark card with a cheerful green leprechaun sitting on a black kettle full of gold coins.

Jim,
I'm mightily pleased with my new collection. So pleased, I've got a little job for you if you want it. Or even if you don't.
The details are outlined in the other envelope, plus funding and some other information you might find of interest.
By the way, thought you might like to have this old Collodion plate for your own collection.
Looking forward to hearing from you.
Stay away from mischief.

- P. F.

It was Israel and Henry. Israel sat in one of those old-timey wicker-backed wheelchairs. He was missing his right leg halfway up the thigh. He looked tired and sick and had lost a hell of a lot of weight. Henry was older — I'd guess fifteen- or maybe even sixteen-years old, but I could already see he was growing into a fine handsome giant of a man. He stood with his hand clapped on his father's shoulder and Israel's opposite hand on top of his. I read the other envelope, packed everything up, and drove all night.

It's a good seven-hour drive from the single-wide down to the Mississippi Delta. I had to stop and ask for directions several times, each new set of clues leading me deeper and deeper into the vast Mississippi River Delta. It's still pretty much the same as it ever was. Level as a new billiard table and blessed with some of the richest soil in the world.

Finally, I found what I was looking for. I was late for services but I slipped into a back pew as quietly as possible. I still caused a little stir; they don't get a lot of lily-white crackers there, but the minister didn't miss a chapter or verse. He had Henry's needle-sharp eyes and dignified bearing. The service was finally over and the minister walked purposely toward me and extended a friendly hand as the congregation watched for trouble.

"Good morning, sir, I am the Reverend Henry Benjamin. I hope you enjoyed the service. What can we do for you?"

"Well, Brother Benjamin, I'm James Broadfoot and I have something for you." I carefully unwrapped the Collodion print and handed it over. "Careful sir, it's quite delicate."

He studied the image for a few moments. "Come with me, Jim. I want you to meet someone."

We walked down the aisle to the front pew where an aged woman sat, surrounded by a protective flock of fierce-looking young men backed by even fiercer-looking women of all ages.

The Reverend knelt and touched the old woman on the arm tenderly. "Mama Lener, this is Mr. Broadfoot, and he's brought you a present."

Her vision might have been murky, but it was good enough. Bright tears began to roll down her weathered Black face, and her lips began to work silently. She shut her eyes for a painfully long time, and I wondered if she was stealing a quick nap.

"It's my daddy and his daddy too. Oh my... oh my. He founded this church, you know."

There wasn't much wind left in her words. I smiled and tried to make the best of it. "Yes, ma'am. I saw that on the sign and I knew I was in the right place. My name's Jim."

She leaned forward in a conspiratorial whisper of surprising intensity. A dark twig of a finger pointed at both faces. "Mr. Jim. He and Grandpa invented the moving picture show."

The Reverend smiled, and I could read the unspoken disclaimer. "Don't mind that. She's been saying that all my life."

"He's buried out back you know," she continued. "Grandpa too. He's the only white man buried in our graveyard."

"Well ma'am, I'd guess he's about the only one who deserves the honor."

Henry took me out back to a small cemetery separated from a sea of young cotton plants by a white picket fence. Israel and Henry Benjamin, inventors of the first motion pictures, lay there next to each other, facing east, awaiting Judgment Day.

Israel had lived until 1879. The elder Henry had founded the little congregation in 1880 and had died surrounded by adoring family in 1930, age one-hundred-one years old.

Reverend Benjamin walked me back to my Mustang. "It's so kind of you to bring the old picture. It means a lot to my family. What exactly is your profession, Mr. Broadfoot?"

I tried to sound nonchalant. "Well, I'm sort of a detective who searches for old pictures and such that are thought to be lost for good."

"I see by your tag you've come a long way to deliver a gift to strangers. Why did you do that?"

"You might say it's an important part of my profession."

He shook my hand as I got into the car. "You're sure you won't stay for Sunday dinner?"

"No sir, I'm off on another search. Just because something waited for a hundred years don't mean it'll wait forever."

"If you don't mind me asking, what are you looking for?"

"The first action photos of sea combat. They were taken during the fight between the CSS Alabama and the USS Kearsarge, just outside Cherbourg Harbor in France. They're definitely known to have existed, but no one's seen them in nearly a century. I've got a client who's provided me with some good leads. I'm pretty sure the images are still out there somewhere."

Now he gave me the sort of wary look that the congregation did when I walked into their church. "You don't strike me as one of those South-shall-rise-again types."

"I'm not; I've just developed a taste for the truth. Let's just say it's a fairly recent development in my life."

"Well good luck with that, Mr. Broadfoot. Sometimes the animal called truth can be as elusive as a unicorn and dangerous as a dragon."

Benjamin had a musically baritone voice. It was easy to imagine it as Henry's voice.

"It is, Reverend, but it's also honest work. Tell you what, when I get back, I'd love to come down and take you up on that Sunday dinner. That all right?"

"Of course, Mr. Broadfoot, you are welcome in our homes anytime."

"And you, sir, are always welcome in mine. You can do me a favor though."

"Of course, what?"

"Call me Jimmy. My real friends call me Jimmy."

He smiled broadly; the man was the spitting image.

"And you may call me Henry. Good luck, Jimmy, and happy landings."

"Goodbye Henry, see you in the funnies."

"We will keep you in our prayers, Jimmy."

"Thanks, I'll need all the help I can get."

Two days later, I landed in Paris and got right down to some good honest work.

THE END

The Salamander

Never go backpacking alone. It's not that I'm trying to inhibit other people from visiting the backcountry, just never, ever, do it alone. Even if you're only moderately well-equipped, backcountry travel is every bit as safe as your average city street, as long as you have a lick of common sense and at least one competent colleague. The difference between the trail and the street is that when you're alone in the backcountry, ten or fifteen miles from the nearest piece-of-shit excuse for a road and you get into trouble, you're on your own. Trip on a snag and puncture a femoral artery? Too bad, you'll probably be dead in about five minutes. Went down to that unspoiled creek to go swimming and all you got was snakebit? I'd say your odds of making it out alive are about fifty-fifty. Made it to the water without getting snakebit but got caught by the current, dragged on the bottom until you were trapped under a logjam with a mouthful of sand? Tough tits pal, no lifeguards out there. Even if the rare, endangered wilderness ranger saw you go under, all he could do about it is file a report. Solo backpacking may have the undeniably romantic overtones of those early pioneers and explorers, but that doesn't mean it's a smart move.

I used to do it all the time. That's how I found Peckerwood Canyon, and that's where I almost met my maker. Peckerwood is only one of a thousand narrow canyons that twist and slice through the bedrock of Tallulah National Forest, and although it is on the map, the contours and elevations are only hurried guesswork. What you don't see on the maps are bottomless pits ringed with Carolina hemlock or the lairs of the last southern panthers that still hunt deer and wild pigs in the lush narrow valleys. A careful examination of the official Department of the Interior topographic map will reveal a small annotation on the bottom border that reads almost like an apology: *This area was mapped by aerial survey - 1950.*

A note like that is enough to give ordinary weekend explorers a thoughtful pause, but to me, it's like an engraved invitation to a wedding with an open bar. That's how I found Peckerwood. About a hundred times before, I just loaded up the 'ole pack and hit the woods till I found an unknown stream flowing into the Tula River, then followed it up to the source, usually a spectacular waterfall or spring that sent its waters tumbling through the last old-growth hardwood forest in the Deep South.

I never found a single canyon that wasn't worth every drop of sweat expended to get in — every one of those unique miniature worlds separated from the rest of the country by twenty miles and ten thousand years. I found one canyon engraved with countless petroglyphs sprawling across towering limestone bluffs like prehistoric road signs. I've discovered about a hundred disintegrating whiskey stills, abandoned the moment prohibition was finally repealed. One thing they all shared in common was traces of human activity. Old shotgun hulls, fire rings, or prehistoric carvings, there's always something. With one exception. I followed a tiny trickle of water uphill to a blowdown of titanic hickory trees blocking the entrance to a narrow valley that somehow, after a lifetime of exploration of the Tallulah, I had never noticed.

It was a real mess, an amalgam of house-sized boulders woven together with centuries of sawbriars and wild grapes. On top of that were the tangled remains of hemlocks and beech trees that had clung tenaciously to life on the bare rock before finally being ripped free by a flood or twisted into an unbreakable net by ever more frequent tornadoes. The whole contorted logjam was coated with carpets of thick moss crowned with ferns and late wildflowers. The other side couldn't be seen, but a steady stream of cold, clear water running from under the plug indicated drainage from a sizeable canyon. The lure of the unknown was irresistible. The Tallulah sprawls over a quarter million acres, and there are canyons big enough to conceal a Rebel ironclad. Once I found jugs of white lightning hidden away on an inaccessible rock ledge, corncob stoppers still in place. The contents had tragically evaporated long before I was born. You just never know until you look — and I always want to look.

Still, despite my addiction to discovery, I was prepared to give it a pass. Clamoring over or squeezing through gaps in the plug would entail risks that I didn't much care for. One miscalculation could result in a shattered femur. This would be followed by a long painful crawl back to find help, provided you didn't die of shock or become dinner for the pigs first. An unwisely chosen handhold could net you a fistful of timber rattler, and we got some real blue ribbon winners down in the Tallulah. I would have given it a pass without a second thought except for one thing: the birds. Pileated woodpeckers to be exact.

They're the closest living relative to the magnificent and very extinct ivory-bill woodpecker. You hear them all the time down in the canyons of the Tallulah, and sometimes, if you're very quiet and very lucky, you can even catch a quick glimpse of one. They're a big bird by woodpecker standards, almost a foot tall with a bright red head and a beak that could open a can of baked beans. Pileated woodpeckers are fairly predictable. They herald the sunrise loud enough to set off car alarms, noisily pound away on insect-infested trees all day, and knock off that work with the same maniacal song. Unless something has happened to its mate, you always find them in pairs, carving out a slice of territory they will defend, even from their own kind, to the bitter end. They are never seen in flocks, but on that late November afternoon, that rule had been thrown out the back door.

There were dozens of them here, swooping and screaming like crows harassing an owl. I dumped my pack and watched them while I ate a snack and indulged in a smoke. Whatever they were up to, it had knocked my presence completely off their radar screen. Ignoring me, they would fly over, then plunge into the hidden canyon like gaudy little fighter jets strafing the living snot out of some unseen enemy, then they would come boiling back out of the canyon to rally in the woods behind me before making another run on the target. Finally, as if on command, they began to pair off and zoom back into the surrounding forest, screeching and calling to each other with the same intense urgency they had shown all afternoon.

Having decided the bizarre display was finally over, I shouldered my pack and was about to head down to the river to camp on a wide sand bar when one last bird landed on the limb of a holly tree not six feet away. Normally, the only time you get that close to one it's because it didn't see you, but this bird definitely knew I was there. We stared at each other for a good five minutes before it squawked loudly and flapped away into the darkening woods, its mysterious behavior as irresistible as a schoolyard dare.

Looking at the sky I decided I had about an hour of usable light. Just enough time to find a way in and set up camp for the night. I tightened the pack straps and began to climb.

I got about halfway up before I began to have serious second thoughts. Two days of steady rain had left the jumble of trees slimy as an oiled flagpole. The higher I went, the harder it got. Finally, a hemlock cracked under my weight, and I fell more than jumped to the narrow ledge of a gigantic limestone boulder. It was a clumsy landing that knocked the air out of my lungs like I'd been sacked by a pair of linebackers. I lay on my back watching the sky and recovering my wind as I slowly began to evaluate my position. Below me, a good thirty-foot drop to a pitiless jumble of rocks. Above me, there was nothing but greasy trees and wet mossy rocks almost impossible to gain a purchase on. I had already decided that discretion was indeed the better part of valor — the best solution was to hole up right here for the night, just haul out the sleeping bag and put my back against the wall to wait for dawn. Then I caught a thin ray of afternoon light streaming through a gap in the rocks. It was laughably narrow, and so tiny under ordinary circumstances that I never would have attempted to get through, but these were not ordinary circumstances.

I had just enough space on the ledge to work my way into the gap, dragging my pack behind me. The passage angled down through dripping seeps of cold water and muddy rocks. Once I saw the unmistakable motion of a snake ducking down into an opening the size of a bathtub drain. I cussed the reptile for moving around so late in the season, sealed the hole with a small slab of rock, then pushed on, goaded by the nasty thought of being snakebit in such an appalling place. My luck held, the snake behaved, and moments later I emerged, bruised, muddy, and exhausted, into Peckerwood Canyon. I've been privileged enough to snorkel the great barrier reefs of Belize and watch the sunrise through the steaming geysers of Yellowstone, but I had never beheld anything as stunningly pristine as this.

It was as pure as a new can of Crisco, with no trails, no fire rings, no cigarette butts — just a long, narrow canyon ringed by gigantic overhanging cliffs fringed with dense thickets of mountain laurel.

There's an old poplar tree on the other side of the forest known rather unimaginatively as The Big Tree that attracts thousands of visitors a year. Its trunk is scarred with the initialed abuse of countless pocketknives wielded by unsupervised scouts and ignorant adults. The Big Tree is surrounded by dozens of fire rings that are slowly cooking the last healthy roots to death. There are always whole trash bags worth of garbage around it, dumped by campers too lazy or stupid to clean up after themselves. One glance at Peckerwood told me that no one had been in here for a long, long time.

There wasn't just one big yellow poplar; there were dozens, each one the size of the abused Big Tree or better, all of them virgins to ax or pocketknife. Shagnut hickories big enough to carve into bass boats stretched up the cliff tops. The ground was a perfect green carpet of ferns unmolested by the roto-tilling of wild pigs. I shouldered my muddy pack and began to carefully pick my way up the canyon between stands of the old-growth timber. No tarnished .22 hulls or faded candy wrappers, no ubiquitous circles of scorched rocks full of charcoal and half-melted aluminum, just a sweet, unspoiled wilderness. Halfway up the canyon, I was hit by a stunning revelation: I had stumbled onto the last unexplored patch of woods in North America. If anyone had been here since Columbus landed, there was no evidence of it.

The air began to cool and the light began to fade the moment the afternoon sun dipped behind the western edge of the canyon. Darkness comes quickly in the bottom of a two-hundred-foot hole. I promptly began scouting for a flat spot to pitch camp. I finally found a suitable location inside a silent cathedral of hemlocks. The sandy ground was mostly free of ferns and saplings. This was a place I could build a small campfire and wipe away the traces when I left. First things first, I stretched out my tent on its lightweight alloy frame and tossed my sleeping bag and pad inside. After hanging my food bag from a convenient limb, I tugged on a pair of old pilot's gloves and headed up to the bottom of the bluff where I could find wood untouched by the recent rains. There wasn't much, just a few branches of mountain laurel as thick as my forearm. It burns like crazy but doesn't have much in the way of legs. You can go through a whole pile of the stuff in just an hour. I began to look for a decent backlog, something the fire could cozy up with for the evening and still have a few coals to start on in the morning.

Peckerwood was a miracle but not a perfect one; every stick of wood on the ground was as rotten as last year's lettuce. Every stick I found was covered with lichens, multicolored mold, and small pallid mushrooms the color of a dead man's face. No problem, if you're an experienced outdoorsy type, you know where to find good wood even after days of drenching rain. Suitable material can be found hanging, caught in the lower branches of trees protected from the damp earth and somewhat sheltered by the canopy above, except in the Peckerwood. The place appeared to have a local ordinance against dry wood; the more I fruitlessly searched, the darker and colder it became. I've hunkered down for the night in many a cold harbor, grateful for a bowl of hot noodles and a dry sleeping bag, but it's definitely not as comfy as a tidy little fire to knock the chill away. I decided to give the base of the bluffs another search. Sometimes the most innocent decisions can lead to the most profound consequences.

I prowled the ancient limestone walls like a famished coyote looking for mice. Something always comes to rest in the lee of the bluff, except down here. I searched until darkness forced me to pull out the headlamp and admit defeat. It would be a chilly night, but not intolerable. The white gas stove would provide a hot meal, and the tent and bag would provide a cozy nest. I've been through worse, camping in my parents' backyard. Still, there's nothing like a friendly blaze when you're alone in the deep dark forest. I began to work my way back along the wall the way I had come when something caught the toe of my boot and sent me sprawling face-first onto the soft rich earth. I indulged in a stream of verbal abuse as I lumbered to my feet, spotting the offending snag poking up through a narrow dry strip of ground. I gave it a vengeful kick, and to my surprise it fairly leapt from the earth. After an experimental tap with my boot, I then bent down to take a closer look. It was a sizable log of dry wood the length of my thigh and twice the thickness, although what sort of tree it had come from was a mystery. The grey color of weathered cedar, it was a mass of knots and swirling grain almost too fine to see with the naked eye. I hefted it up with both hands and was pleasantly surprised to feel how heavy it was. Dense woods like hickory and oak are the most desirable firewood because of the large amount of energy they contain. A few logs of decent hardwood will outlast and outheat twice their weight in soft pine. Grunting with effort, I began to make my way down the slope toward camp, stopping every twenty or thirty feet to drop my burden and rest my aching arms.

It was past sundown when I finally came dragging the log into camp. I flopped down to catch my breath. The damned thing was a lot heavier than it looked, but I had decided it would be well worth the effort, as the chilly evening damp began to really seep in.

I set the log on a small patch of bare earth I had prepared earlier and built a bird's nest of mountain laurel in a shallow depression on top of the wood. It wasn't much, but a little bit of something beats the hell out of a whole lot of nothing. I reached into the front pocket of my ratty green field jacket and dug out my lighter. One of those cheapo plastic butane jobs whose short-lived relatives crowd dumps and landfills around the globe. Turned out, this one was ready for the boneyard too, not even a spark for encouragement. No problem. I always keep a backup in the stove's little nylon case for such occasions. Except this time. No reason to panic, a good outdoorsman always carries triple backup for fire, and mine was a pack of matches tucked away in my first-aid kit. They were there all right, their damp red heads crumbling and useless. Stashed in an outer pouch of my pack, the matches had been dosed in chilly water during the epic muddy struggle through the plug.

I was wet, cold, and fuming over the lapse of my expertise, but mightily grateful there was no one to witness it. After all, I had a reputation to protect. I went through every waterproof bag in my pack and came up with bone-dry Band-Aids, Chap Stick, clean underwear, and dry socks, but no matches. I shouted in frustration to the lonely canyon. My words echoed back at me like I was being mocked by some smart-ass kid.

"How can I be lugging around a thousand dollars' worth of gear but not a single damn kitchen match!"

The words faded along with the last of the late daylight while another crop of goosebumps spread over my arms and legs. I fumed and thought bitterly about all the jokers on survival shows kindling blazes with an incredible assortment of materials: coconut fiber, bamboo, headlights, and 12-volt batteries. Well, there were no car batteries down here and coconut trees were about as common as short-faced bears. On the outside chance there might have been something I had forgotten, I dug out the repair kit in the bottom of the pack. Even to light the stove I had to produce a spark for ignition. There was a small roll of duct tape wound around an empty thread spool, a sleeping pad and tent patches, eyeglasses repair kit, but no matches. Finally, my fingers closed around a small slab of a cold metallic rectangle. I held it up in the fading light of my headlamp and indulged myself in a surge of hope.

It was one of those bits of survival gear you can haul across a continent and use so little that it remains forgotten and unused in a corner of the pack until the day you hang up your boots for good. It's a half-ounce block of magnesium with a long flint striker embedded along one edge. The silver-white metal burns with a hellish intensity, provided, as the old joke goes, you can get it lit. Here's how it's allegedly supposed to work: you shave or scrape a small pile of magnesium shavings into a little pile at the base of your intended fire. Then you use a knife blade, preferably crafted from high carbon steel, to shower sparks from the striker onto your pile of metallic kindling. It sounds easier than it is in practice.

It might not be so demanding in the backyard on a sunny day, but it's a little more challenging in the bottom of a deep, dark, wet hole in the Earth, working with fingertips numb from the cold.

It was painstaking work; magnesium is harder than aluminum and doesn't give up without a fight. The longer I worked, the duller the blade became. I consoled myself with the thought of sitting by my hard-won blaze, leisurely whetting the knife to "shaving sharp" with the little diamond rod clipped to the scabbard. Finally, after what seemed like an hour's work, I produced a small mound of the volatile metal about the size of my little finger, piled into a small depression on the backlog. After carefully arranging a pile of laurel twigs around the filaments of magnesium, I reversed the block and smacked the striker with a sharp hard blow. The old-fashioned carbon steel did me right. There was a shower of blinding white sparks, but no flare of burning metal.

I huddled closer to the tinder. A chilly wind began to stir the canyon as colder air sought out the lowest point on the landscape. The headlamp expired before I could line up for a second strike. Firing by guess and by God, I could see the fog of my breath, illuminated like a cloud of neon gas, by the cascade of hot sparks. My heart sank as sparks bounded off the pile like it was made of salt. Then I suddenly caught the hint of a small glow that rapidly expanded into a volcano of intense white fire. I was so surprised by the lightning-sharp oxidation of the magnesium that I almost forgot to pile on more tinder. The laurel hissed and popped into bright yellow light. I was stingy with the wood. There wasn't much, and I was determined to make it last.

The sides of the shallow depression that held the tiny fire began to glow with the deep red heat of a stove element. The red patch began to spread as it began to wick out an oily-looking liquid that burned like sand soaked with gasoline. Lighting my stove with a flaming twig, I adjusted the burner and put on a kettle of water. I studied my backlog as the water began to heat. It was still burning with an unabated intensity. There was no sign of the resin (or whatever it was that was running out) of even slowing down. To the contrary, it was definitely gaining power. Sitting four or five feet away, I could feel the heat radiating through to my toes as the boot fabric began to steam. Grateful beyond words for the simple blessing of fire, I opened a small bottle of single malt scotch and flicked a few drops from my fingers onto the hungry Earth, then took a long deep pull for me.

I concluded that the burning log was the heart of a stump, probably from a white pine or red cedar, that had been curing in the dusty lee of the limestone wall for decades or even centuries. I began to feel a little guilty. It had lain there slowly dissolving into its constituent elements for God knows how long, and here I came along and set it on fire. I took another pull and capped the bottle, saving the rest for after dinner, and shrugged off the uncomfortable thought. But a certain creeping unease remained. After the water began to boil, I trimmed the burner down to a low blue ring of heat and dumped in a pouch of noodles. As I ate my dinner, I watched the log with growing curiosity.

The log was generating so much heat that I had to keep backing away to enjoy my dinner. A steady blaze continued to burn unabated in the shallow depression, but here and there I could see bright red flecks burning through twisted knotholes and needle-slim fissures in the wood. Finishing my noodles, I walked a few feet to the narrow stream that flowed through the heart of the Peckerwood and scrubbed the dented stainless steel kettle thoroughly with sand.

I was scrubbing away the last of the sticky noodles with a sharp quartz pebble when it dawned on me how well I could see this far from the fire. The log was now glowing like a white-hot horseshoe as bits of the surface began to fall away and sizzle on the ground like white phosphorous.

Concerned for the safety of my nylon tent, I extracted the stakes from the ground and moved it a little farther away from the intensifying blaze. After a moment of sober reflection, I hefted up the pack and leaned it against a gigantic beech tree behind the tent. I uncapped the bottle of scotch again and treated myself to a few swigs, then an after-dinner smoke. I sat down to study a fire that needed no tending or replenishment of fuel.

I've always seen fascinating apparitions living in the hearts of campfires. I've sat up until dawn on occasions, hypnotized by visions of cliff dwellings inhabited by glowing people or fantastic animals contentedly grazing in fields of red-hot coals. But I always knew these were projections of my own mind.

This fire's coals, however, were something new. I began to see forms being etched out of the backlog. Nothing I could put my finger on. Hints of limbs and the arc of a backbone curling around it like a boa constrictor squeezing out rivulets of searing goo that seemed to set the sand on fire. I finished the bottle and lit another smoke. I had intended to turn in, but now decided the smart money would be to sit up for a while until there were enough ashes to bank the fire until morning. I began to spy little squashed faces and twisted trees as flakes of the log began to fall away and burn on the barren sand. There was a loud pop as a hunk of blazing wood the size of a silver dollar spalled off to almost land in my lap.

I laughed and scrambled back, then I saw something that wiped that idiotic smile right off of my face. There was a tiny black reptilian hand trying to claw its way out of the flaming log. My heart sank. I had murdered a hibernating lizard or some other creature by using its home as firewood. My friends had often teased me about my somewhat contradictory approach to wildlife and life in general. I'll move a caterpillar off the trail to keep it from getting crushed by clueless hikers. I'll murder a wild sow and leave her brutish children for the bobcats without a trace of remorse. I've been known to stop and help a migrating turtle cross the road at a risk to my own life, but settle down to a hearty bowl of venison stew that very evening. I sighed with very real regret. There was nothing I could do but watch the creature get fried alive, and at the same time be intrigued that it had lasted this long.

I waited for the poor thing to finally break free in a blind panic, sizzling to death in the open while I watched. It only took a few moments of observation to conclude that whatever it was, it wasn't in any big hurry. The tiny hand flexed its glistening fingers as more bits of wood fell away to reveal a muscular forearm. Then I could see the flank of the thing contract and expand as it took deep regular breaths of superheated air with no visible signs of distress. The creature became more active and clawed at its fiery prison. More hunks of wood dropped away as it began to dig its way out. Sliding free of the log, it flopped to the smoldering ground where I expected to see it twist and convulse with the agony of being burned alive. It was a large black salamander. It was no more concerned than a cat napping in the afternoon sun.

There are old wives tales about salamanders who live in fire, but the legends are as baseless as hoop snakes and as ridiculous as jackalopes. No, like Lincoln had once famously said, 'Son, you got your facts absolutely right, but you're drawing the wrong conclusion.' It only happened because a fishmonger's wife had thrown a mostly rotten log on the fire and the poor hibernating critter had woken up with its bedroom in flames. Well, this was no rotten log, I wasn't an illiterate peasant, and this sure as hell was no ordinary salamander. The closer I looked the more it became obvious that the creature bore only a rough resemblance to the ancient line of amphibians. Beneath a skin that shimmered like hot tar, you could clearly see its well-defined musculature. The hind legs were rather ordinary, but the forelimbs were eerily human-like. It processed five-fingered hands that slowly clenched and relaxed like someone trying to restore circulation to a sleeping limb.

Its skull was more iron wedge than delicate bone lattice. I could see the thin trace of a permanent smile carved along the lower jaw. Its eyes were sheltered by crusty, hard-looking lids. The fire had begun to subside a little, and the salamander struggled closer to the intense heat, shoving a path under the flaming log with its sharp slab of a head. Its reaction was the direct opposite of any ordinary creature. It wasn't fleeing the heat; it was seeking it out. Out of curiosity, I tossed a small bundle of laurel on the fire that shot up leaping yellow tongues of flame. The creature whipped around with rattlesnake speed and instantly pinned me down with glittering hot eyes. It studied me intensely for a few seconds. The trap-like jaws slowly opened and it began to sing.

Imagine the keening drone of bagpipes taken upwards to the edge of human hearing. A frequency that shivers leaves off limbs and then blows them away with the energy of a gas-powered leaf blower. It was a sound that should have forced me to clamp both hands over my ears and open my mouth to equalize the pressure. But it didn't. There was something in the frequency that made you want to lean in close. When you did, you could detect subtle, almost sub-sonic frequencies that made it even more intriguing. I shook my head in disbelief. I wouldn't have been any more amazed if the creature had put on a straw boater and belted out "Michigan Rag" while tap dancing. The fire began to die back. The song began to fade like a tape player with old batteries. I didn't know much about the creature at this point, but there was one thing I knew for sure: it wanted more fire.

The rest of the dry wood, no more than a big armful, went into the fire. Saving wood at night to fight off the chill of dawn is a thoroughly ingrained backcountry habit that pays big dividends. Like washing your hands after a trip to the cat hole or treating every drop of drinking water. I suppose that's the moment the salamander began to get its hooks into my brain, but I couldn't have cared less. Fuel made it sing and I wanted to hear more. The wood had only been on the fire for a few blinks of the eye when it all went up in a simultaneous flash. No smoke, no steam, just an intense blast of heat that forced me to reflexively shield my face and jump away. The smell of charred cloth plus a searing blast of pain around my wrists told me I had been a little too close.

I angrily patted out the smoldering cuffs of my field jacket and, like many men, spoke in anger before thinking much about what I was saying. “You little sumbitch! You like to burn my ass up!” I was just beginning to examine second-degree burns where the skin had been exposed between the gloves and sleeves when a thought that was not my own rang inside my head — a sledgehammer on a church bell.

“Give me more.”

The creature was sitting on a tripod of tail and hind legs staring directly at me with eyes of freshly crystalized obsidian. I looked at the surrounding woods for whoever had followed me into this hidden place. The likelihood that someone had tailed me into this secret canyon was somewhere between slim to none. I shouted into the darkness anyway. I’ve never been afraid of the dark or the rustle of an unknown creature in the woods, just highly respectful. Now, despite the heat, I felt a shiver of cold fear.

“Who’s there?”

There was only silence and the crackling of the fire. The voice rang out between my ears once more.

“Give me more.”

Stepping as close to the fire as I dared, I saw the creature had changed; it was thicker now and the skin had an aura of flickering white light that could be seen through the flames. The eyes were brighter, its pupils glittering diamonds, its tiny teeth intense little jets of blinding white plasma. I couldn’t decide what to do, so I played dumb.

“Give you more what?”

The answer was loud enough to shatter cast iron.

“More!”

I held up my arms and showed it the rings of scorched flesh encircling my wrists.

“Look what you did to my arms, you little monster! Why should

I give you anything? I ought to give you a bucket of cold water!"

Opening its jaws, it lifted its iron head and began to sing.

Now it was my sixth birthday party. Both my parents were alive, my father's cancer still a future nightmare, and my mother still attractive with the joy of life gleaming in her eyes. All my friends from school were around me, stuffing their innocent faces with cake and ice cream. There was a rustle of excitement as my Uncle Julian brought in a cardboard box and sat it next to my chair. Looking down, I saw a pair of tiny brown paws scrape at the top of the box and heard the distinctive yip. It was the dog that would be my best friend until it died of heartworms and old age on my twenty-first birthday. It was Puppy. I reached down into the box, patted its silky head, and was rewarded by frantic licking. Mother lifted it out of the box and placed the mutt into my arms.

Puppy. The salamander had returned my long-dead dog to me. The indomitable, infuriating, and absolutely loyal Pup had returned. I kissed it on the head and held it to my chest. Then it was gone, and I was staring at the salamander. The tears running down both my cheeks evaporated in the heat as I made the most momentous decision of my life.

"All right, whatever the hell you are, I'll feed you, but it's going to be an even trade, right? I'll give you what you don't have and you pay me in kind. Deal?"

"More … now!"

"Yeah, I'll give you more. Keep your britches on. I'll see what I can find."

I prowled the woods within the circle of light, grabbing wood I had rejected out of hand only a few hours earlier. Returning to the fireside, I carefully laid a half-rotten log across the glowing remains of the salamander's cocoon.

"Sorry it's wet … "

A billowing cloud of hot steam snatched the words away from my mouth. The half-decayed wood burst into an intense blaze, and small multi-legged creatures, dashed from their sleep by the heat, stumbled into hell, sublimated instantly into puffs of white vapor. The salamander tilted its head toward the murky sky and began to sing once more. The unearthly song hummed with an effortless power that reached deep into my brain and began to tease out random pleasures — biting into ice-cold watermelon on a searing July day, or falling exhausted into a soft bed made with clean sheets. It was nice, but I knew it could provide more. If it could reach back into memories nearly forty years old, events that only I had the dimmest recollection of, it could provide much more.

I stumbled through the damp canyon groping for more wood. I wondered if I should attempt to capture it. It was just small enough to fit into my stainless steel kettle. It was plausible that I could scoop it up with the small trowel of the same metal. Then a sobering thought: the creature had power. It wouldn't likely appreciate, or tolerate, being scooped up like a net full of minnows destined to bait a trotline.

Dragging back the wet carcass of a hickory, I determined to be careful with my thoughts. As I approached the fire, it quit the song and just watched me with a bottomless gaze. I placed the log next to the amphibian. As before, steam flushed out a thousand confused critters that in their turn went up in smoke. I got down as close as I could, shielding my face with one arm. I noticed a sleeve was beginning to smolder.

"All right, there you are. Where's mine?"

It stared in silence. The powerful-looking jaws were still curved into a permanent grin, but the creature's mood had somehow changed. I was keeping my end of the bargain, but the damned thing just sat there immobile and silent as a fire hydrant. I scuttled a few inches closer, close enough to feel the skin on my cheeks begin to peel away like the dried skin of an onion. The salamander had cracked the door of paradise open a few inches. What I wanted now was for that door to fly open. In frustration, I poked it with a lichen-covered stick.

"Well, do something, damnit!"

Now, fat drops of cold rain mixed with stinging balls of hail pounded my head and shoulders. Looking across the parking lot, I could see a boiling black cloud, held together with tremendous bolts of lightning, flow out of a low range of hills only two miles away. The storm surged downhill to gobble up an eighteen-hole golf course as people around me began to scream and run for cover. The fear filled my mouth with the taste of raw brass, making it impossible to shout. I stood transfixed as the tornado spun toward me, unstoppable as a tsunami. The wall cloud stomped across the interstate, throwing cars and tractor-trailer rigs with the ease of an angry child abusing its toys. A cement truck, its mixer still rotating, bounced into the parking lot like a loose football. Its driver was flung out of the cab to die, impaled on the shattered end of a wooden telephone pole. The truck skidded to a stop on its side only a hundred feet away, grey concrete flowed out of the ruptured mixer like thick lumpy blood. The storm bore down on me with god-like fury, and I dashed into the grocery store for cover.

Screams and absolute blackness that made hell look like Waikiki Beach. The roof crashed in, burying the back half of the store and dozens of people under tons of steel and roofing. There was the gentle patter of rain mixed with the moans of the crushed and broken. I heard the faraway howl of a single siren, then more and more, like hungry wolves closing in from all sides. Standing up, I gawked at the open sky as trailing flashes of electricity illuminated my surroundings. I was standing over a woman whose chest had been smashed by a cash register. She looked at me with pleading eyes as blood foamed into dark bubbles on her broken lips. Then the darkness returned. Stumbling toward the glow of blazing gas mains, I left her to die in the dark, on the floor of the produce department, alone and terrified.

Then I was back. Sitting in the almost unbearable heat as the salamander's thoughts bounced around inside my skull.

"Yours for mine yours for mine yours for mine … "

I held up one trembling hand.

"All right, you got me. Look, it was never a serious idea. I won't try to catch you. I'll give you whatever you want. I promise if you won't hurt me, I won't hurt you. Deal? No more bad memories … please."

The hickory was going fast, and I began to prowl the woods under giant shadows cast on the pale limestone bluffs. Everything that I could carry or drag back to the fire was consumed by the salamander as it keened out an increasingly intense song. Its mouth began to radiate like a welder's electric arm as it lifted its head toward the unseen stars above. I stepped and fetched for hours, my only reward the ethereal song of the salamander. The fuel began to run low. I brought in smaller and smaller pieces of wood, some so rotten they fell apart in my blistering hands. The salamander's shining black skin was now speckled with white-hot dots. Its song began to fade as the fuel was consumed. The ringing of a single iron word inside my head.

"More! More! More!"

Out of desperation, I threw in clumps of damp organic matter scooped from the forest floor. Each handful vaporized instantly. Through shimmering waves of heat, I watched a small limestone pebble crumble into lime. The salamander wasn't getting enough and I knew it, but enough for what? I stopped feeding the fire for a quick moment.

"Why do you need this? What's the point of all this effort?"

The hot glass eyes pinned me to the spot as the song faded away. Then, another single word, a single thought really, burst between my ears and behind my eyes.

"Thermogenesis."

With more handfuls of organic matter mixed with sand and pebbles, the sand began to sag and dissolve into tiny puddles of lava. Quartz pebbles glowed like atomic fireflies. The salamander scooped a pebble between its jaws, crunching down with no more effort than eating a potato chip. It was still changing; the body, tail and legs began to shine with a mottled golden pattern. A small lump had broken through the skin on top of its head. I watched the lump grow into a half-polished diamond as I threw in any material within reach. By now the front and sleeves of my old field jacket were charred black, and the hair on my face had crinkled away to carbon stubble. It still wasn't enough. Then I had an inspiration and held out the block of magnesium. The salamander watched me with the focus of a dog being teased with a bone, and I knew I had him.

My scorched lips hurt like hell when I spoke.

"Sing for me some more … no … show me something … show me something good, and it's all yours. We got a bargain, remember — you do for me and I'll —"

A wave of hot sonic power swept me back to Nashville, Tennessee and my first woman. Oh, I had been parking and made out, fumbled around and been fumbled with a hundred times, but she was the first woman who ever gave her body to me. The first one I had who knew exactly what she was doing and was willing to show me what to do. I was nineteen, in Bible college, and struggling to resolve the Christian fundamentalist view of the world with the reality I was beginning to discover outside the church. She was nearly old enough to be my mother, a statuesque, red-headed beauty married to a mouse-like minister who, as it turned out, didn't pay near enough attention to her.

I was embracing her naked body once more as we tumbled onto a mattress on the floor. I could smell her, taste her and feel the swish of thick auburn hair across my face as she rode me like the great Whore of Babylon. I wanted to stay there forever, but the salamander brought me snapping back like a broken bungee cord. I awoke from the spell sitting inside a blackened circle of ground with my back against a steaming hemlock. I had an erection so intense it hurt. The salamander shouted inside my head. It was like being dosed with a combination of vodka laced with LSD and then thrown off the roof of your house. Something hard pressed painfully into the palm of my right hand; I looked down and saw I still had the block of magnesium. The fireproof pilot's gloves were crumbling like old newsprint.

"More! Thermogenesis! More!"

I staggered as near to the fire as I dared. Now the salamander wore a brilliant diamond embedded between its eyes. Its entire body glowed like molten gold. My speech was slurred and broken, and I was aware that it was affecting my nervous system, but by this point I didn't give a damn. It was my turn to pony up. I held the block of highly reactive metal between my blistered thumb and forefinger and pointed at it with my other hand.

"That was pretty good. Tell you what, little fella, I give you this and you'll take me back, right? I want you to take me way down, as deep as you can. Deal?"

I tossed the block toward the fire, and the creature snatched it from the air with iridescent jaws lined with teeth of electric arcs. It chomped down on the metal bar which instantly burst into a blinding white light. In a cloud of sparks, it broke the striker bar like a breadstick and began to lap up the flaming liquid metal. After the last drop was gone, the salamander licked its chops, lifted its glowing golden head, and began to sing. Faithful and true to our agreement, I was taken far down and far back.

I pressed my calloused hand into the print left in the soft dirt by our quarry. Its stride was beginning to shorten, the limp was getting worse, and it couldn't last much longer. I shielded my eyes and looked back over the arid land at the tribe following behind. Only the weakness from starvation could force our tribe to string out like that. The strongest and youngest were in the front; the oldest members were only a speck back on the horizon. It was an impossibly vulnerable place to be. Unless the stragglers caught up by sundown, the night would claim them for its own. I looked carefully at the tracks; the edges were still sharp despite the constant dry wind. We were getting closer.

The big question now was: would our strength last long enough to make a big kill before we dropped from malnutrition and dehydration? My younger brother was sitting on an empty termite mound, his head hanging between his legs like a broken doll. I hauled him to his feet and sent him ahead before detailing two other hunters back to the rear to collect as many as they could. One man, an older cousin with one eye grown permanently shut from a forgotten injury, nodded and began to stagger back, propped up by a heavy thrusting spear. The other, brought in from another band several seasons before, only glared at me from under a thick shelf of bone that shadowed his eyes. Trade-In had always been sullen. He had only been getting worse as times got harder.

I hated to expend the energy, but I hated having him behind me even worse. He glowered at me, and looked back toward the women and children, then swung at my head with a hand as I ducked away with reflexes honed by a lifetime of living in a world with no farms or villages. The sharp flint ripped out a hunk of my scalp as I slipped one ankle behind his leg and shoved hard. The challenger tumbled to the ground in a cloud of red dust, bounced up, and came at me again with his ax raised high over his shaggy head. I met him with the thrower, smashing the curved wood against his forearm as it came down to split open my face. There was a sickening wet pop as the bone snapped.

I gave him a few seconds to contemplate the gravity of such an injury, then I slashed at his throat with such force that the wooden edge tore the junction between his massive jaw and buffalo neck, releasing a stream of bright red blood with enough force to paint my face crimson. I watched the light fade from his eyes as he lay face up, still not quite able to believe I had bested him so suddenly and with such finality. By the time everyone had caught up, he had quit twitching, and flies were already crawling over his ugly face.

Everyone stood staring at the rotten bastard while saliva rolled down their chins. I knew what they were thinking and I would have none of it.

I pushed them into motion. We left the challenger's body for the scavengers.

I kept glancing at the smoldering sun as it slipped closer and closer to the horizon. We didn't have much time. Whether we could move on in the morning after another hungry night was anyone's guess. Finally, I came up on the scouts who were hunkered down behind a brittle clump of scrub that stank loudly of creosote. The youngest hunter, Handsome, a popular and perpetually good-natured fellow, pointed at what looked to be a huge termite mound several hundred yards away. The wind suddenly shifted to our backs, and the "mound" rose and began to limp away, dragging the right hind leg like an injured friend. I patted Handsome on the shoulder and nodded in approval. I wondered how long I would be able to conceal my diminishing vision from the others. I squinted at the injured fork-horn deer and could make out the stub of a thrusting spear still poking out of its haunch. We might have been near the end of our tether, but one look at the stumbling animal and I knew its luck might run out first.

Despite its crippling wounds, taking down the fork-horn would require a combination of finesse and boldness. It had already killed one man. That, plus the elimination of the immediate competition, had reduced the available hunters by two. In a group totaling no more than the normal number of fingers and toes, the loss was potentially catastrophic. Coupled with the drought and the scarcity of any kind of game, it wouldn't take much more to push us over the edge into the abyss. Fork-horns were dimwitted brutes with sour dispositions. They were rarely hunted, and for several good reasons.

The animals were harder to kill than a cave bear. You could chase a cave bear off the edge of a cliff with fire and noise, but a fork-horn was too stupid to be afraid. They were as blind as worms but made up for it with a keen sense of smell. The animal seemed to glory in a spiteful twist to its personality. They were known to trample a hunter into a gooey paste before crapping and pissing on the flattened remains, then come back after a good feed and do it again. A fork-horn would batter the refuge of a treed enemy until the tree came down or the animal broke its head. There wasn't the first streak of fat in their muscle, and the damn things didn't even taste good.

No one had seen one or even heard of one for a long, long time. Everything I knew about the fearsome beast was learned as a child, sitting on my mother's lap after a big trade feast, listening in awe at the lies and legends being swapped by men around the fire. My father's father, on his first big hunt, was with a band of hunters that tricked one into a pitfall, then couldn't quite figure out what to do with the thing. No one had the guts to jump in the hole and shove a spear through its eye, and the heaviest rocks they could manage just bounced off its skull. Finally, deciding that they would starve before the fork-horn, they left it and went to find some wood, planning to cook the troublesome beast in situ, horns and all. A while later they came back but the animal was gone, replaced by the freshly trampled remains of what might have been a lion. Men debated for years how the animal had escaped and the lion got stomped flat. But no satisfactory explanation was ever floated.

A few more years, and it would have been out of living memories altogether. We were close enough now to spread out in a semicircle, gradually taking up positions on both flanks, too close to ignore and too far to charge. The goal was to keep it moving til it collapsed from exhaustion. The sun bloated like a dead elephant and turned the color of old blood far out on the horizon. The closer we got, the more detail I could make out. A single horn on its broad nose that branched out into two blunt points, each one broad as a big man's foot is long. Absurdly small eyes, fluttering hairy ears the size of water gourds, and nostrils big enough to put your fist into. I could see the broad rows of scars left by the attack of a lion running down its rump. The big cat must have been pretty hard up to tackle this brute. Hard up as we were now. A thought hit me at that moment: could this be the same animal that had escaped my father's father? It was possible. Everyone knew snakes and turtles never just died on their own. No, the hairless only died when something killed one. You could tell it had led a pretty exciting life; I could see its history traced on its thick brown hide — other lion attacks, bush fires, and fighting over women of his own kind. There were even a few crumpled scars that looked like old spear wounds.

The fork-horn turned and sniffed the air. I hadn't been there at the first encounter, and I had taken descriptions of its size with a lick of salt. Even a canecutter looks bigger than a warthog when it's running right at you, but I was close enough now to see that the tales had been no exaggeration. It was taller than I could reach into the sky. I stopped, and the rest of the group held in place, watching me for cues. I was still trying to figure out what to do when it snorted and spun away, trotting over the dusty ground at a respectable speed. Then it did something truly remarkable for such a huge beast: it dropped out of sight quicker than a startled groundhog.

We all stood there giving each other shrugs and stupid looks. Was this some forgotten or unknown trick the behemoth used to survive? Could it turn itself invisible? I stuffed my unease back down; this was no time for hesitation. Extending the arc into a loose circle, we began to creep forward to close the noose, ready for anything. The plan of attack had been agreed upon days ago. It was simple and direct: blind the animal and take him down. There was only a rush of blood through my ears and the soft squeak of sand under my feet as I went forward. I was nearly ready to jump out of my hair. Where in the hell was it?

Then I caught a muffled bellow, more distress than anger. We moved forward, still cautious, and despite our desperate condition, itching with curiosity. Handsome found it first. I could see him smile and wave us toward him with a slender throwing spear. We all laughed when we found the fork-horn. It had stumbled into one of those deep sinkholes that dot the countryside and now stood hip-deep in muck, surrounded by crumbling gravel cliffs, bellowing about the unfairness of it all. We all felt joy for the first time in a season and clapped each other on the shoulders. I turned toward two more men to wave them back to help gather up the women and kids. The quicker we brought in the stragglers, the better.

Now the sky was shifting to a deep purple as the moon took her place in the night sky. I walked over to Handsome to congratulate him on a job well done. The famous smile shone like polished ivory in the moonlight. Then the smile vanished and his spear came up as something smacked into me from behind. Tumbling face-first onto the warm dust, I rolled over, searching frantically for my lost hardwood thrower. I looked up, expecting a bear or leopard that must have stalked us, waiting for the big kill before driving us away. When I saw what had bowled me over, I was completely flabbergasted. It was Trade-In, and the bastard looked pretty lively for a dead man with a busted arm. Well, whatever his other faults might have been, lack of physical toughness wasn't among them. Black clotted blood plastered his long red hair to his face and neck, and the wound I had dealt him was closed with clumps of dust and spider webs. One arm dangled swollen and useless. His good hand was filled with a large unworked piece of stone.

He came for me with a croaking shout, the sharp stone held high. I scrabbled back a few feet and flung a handful of dust at Trade-In's bearish face. He shrieked and reflexively ducked back, giving me enough room to lurch to my feet. Half-blinded, Trade-In lunged forward and we locked up before I could yank my knife free. The blade was good black glass from better times. If I could get at it, I'd skin the selfish little shit alive and take my time about it. We struggled for a moment over the stone and the knife. He smashed his forehead into my mouth, and my head was in a cloud of singing birds and bright dancing stars. Still gripping him by both arms, we plunged into the sinkhole, landing directly in front of the fork-horn.

On my back in the hot black mud, I saw Handsome look down over the edge at us, his mouth wide with surprise. We locked eyes for a second. He was a good man, and even if the drought broke soon or we found a better place, they would need him more than me. Trade-

In, on the other hand, was a sorry, worthless excuse for a human. Whatever his woman had seen in him was a mystery to us all. He was rude, pushy and always scheming to get out of work. He hadn't even made a new baby. The fork-horn let loose with a tremendous snort followed by a bellow that triggered a small avalanche of dirt and rocks into the pit. I looked for Trade-In. He was a few feet away struggling to push himself up from the mud with one good arm. The fork-horn lurched toward us, battling against the slimy ground with everything it had left. He had us marked, and by the Big Blue Bowl of the All-Powerful Sky, he would stomp us deep into the earth if it was the last thing he ever did.

I lurched up and fell onto Trade-In's back, shoving his face down into the muck with both hands. He kicked and thrashed like a trapped antelope. The fork-horn thundered a little closer and my vision began to blink on and off. The pain in my side was nearly unbearable. I could feel the hot breath of the fork-horn behind me. My head began to spin like holy spirals on sacred rocks. Then the blackness of the deep caverns. I awoke next to a happy fire of dried dung. Strips of meat sizzled on the rocks, and Handsome was still there, rewarding me with his big smile when he saw I was awake.

There was the wind of excited words through camp, and a small crowd gathered — stoic women and frightened children. They must have been eating; everyone looked better already. Myself, I had no appetite at all, just an all-consuming thirst. There was a shout of triumph nearby, and several people rushed away. I sipped a little brackish water from a gourd held to my lips.

It felt better than happy water going down. Old Cactus Girl patted warm water onto my forehead.

"Handsome got down in the hole with the rope under his arms and we hauled you both out before you got squashed."

I couldn't talk; I could only ask with my eyes. Handsome gestured back down toward the pit.

"Trade-In and the fork-horn share the same grave. What you said was true. The beast stomped and butted until it finally fell dead. You were wrong about one thing though; it doesn't taste so bad."

More shouts and excitement. Handsome looked up and nodded with approval.

"Finally, some honest wood and good meat. I'm grateful to the Big Blue Bowl of the All-Powerful Sky for anything we have, but I sure get tired of grasshoppers cooked over a fire of dried shit. Might just be me, but so far the beast tastes pretty good."

It hurt to laugh. We clasped hands and I suddenly felt like I could sleep until the next nest of time. I knew my season was running out fast, but somehow, knowing Handsome would step into my place and Trade-In was gone forever, I was left with a sense of inner peace I had never felt. A shower of red sparks climbing high turned my head toward the fire. New Cactus Girl and Moon Owl tossed on a large log of strange grey wood with an impossibly fine grain knotted into twisted little faces. The log flared up with an intense heat, forcing people to suddenly jump back, half-laughing and half-shouting with alarm.

Everyone gathered close to watch the log burn until a small black hand began to scrape its way out from the inside. Someone threw on a bundle of brush followed by dried dung and anything else that would burn. A stumpy black creature finally dropped out of its hiding place and then stretched in the fire the way a lion stretches after a long nap in the sun. It lifted its iron head and began to sing.

Then I was back in the Peckerwood, sitting far too close to the fire. The blaze had settled down into an intensely hot puddle of slag. The salamander sat in the center of the heat, content as a frog in a mud puddle. For a while, I just sat there and watched deep black shadows dance with brilliant white light on the canyon walls, listening to the salamander hum and coo contentedly. I felt drunker and more confused than ever now. A growing pain eating at my toes finally got so bad that I peeked down to see that my boots had been reduced to charred leather and melted rubber. Imported from Switzerland and custom-fitted in the store, they had cost me half a week's pay. Normally I would have been outraged at the unnecessary destruction of expensive gear, but now it didn't seem important at all. I spoke to the salamander with the slurred voice of a severe head injury.

"That was pretty wild. You didn't just make that up, did you?"

The salamander contemplated me for a moment, then lapped up the few remaining drops of molten metal. The words rang in my head louder than ever.

"Yours for mine! More! More now! Thermogenesis now!"

I nodded and began to crawl on my hands and knees back to my gear. Given enough energy, aluminum burns like the fires of hell, and so does steel. The nylon tent and pack fabric drooped limply over their frames like half-cooked taffy. Gritting my teeth against the pain of fried hands, I clumsily began to slice away the nylon with my knife and tossed the lightweight tent poles and pack frame into the fire. Within seconds, the salamander sucked it all down in dazzling waves of pure white light. Almost as an afterthought, I tossed in my treasured knife. Now it somehow had lost its importance. The salamander grabbed it by the tip and worried it down as the leather grips burst into greasy black smoke. Now the golden skin was far too bright to look at directly, but glancing sideways, I could see it lift its jeweled head and howl the terrible, beautiful song.

"More. More. Thermogenesis now."

I sat on my butt and spread my hands helplessly.

"I'm all tapped out. All tapped out."

The creature found this an unacceptable excuse; it glared at me for a few moments and began to jackhammer my brain.

"MoreMoreMoreMore!"

I looked around in desperation at the blackened circle of hemlocks, then caught a reflection of something half-hidden in shadow. It was the white gas stove and the one-liter bottle I carried extra fuel in. The stove was empty but the bottle was full, and for some reason hadn't exploded from the heat. I crawled to the bottle and grubbed it up between my ruined hands. Putting my back to the tree, I was able to push myself upright and hold up the stainless steel bottle. My arms were black with the charred remains of my jacket and shirt.

"This is all that's left. Take it."

With those words, I awkwardly tossed the bottle into the gleaming pool of boiling sand. The salamander grappled with the bottle as I dumbly watched its hands and mouth melt into the hardened steel alloy. I came to myself for a fleeting instant and tried to back away, but it was too late. There was a blinding flash of atomic light. Clamping my hands over my eyes, I was amazed to see the red bones of my fingers shining through my eyelids, then the blackness and silence of deep caverns.

I woke up completely wet and shivering cold, face up in the shallow stream that divides Peckerwod Canyon down the center. Blurred but colorful shapes swooped and dived through the fuzzy woods above me, jabbering at each other in their hysterical language. One giant woodpecker landed a few feet over my head, and we studied each other until it squawked and flapped away. It was a long time before I was able to prop myself up on one elbow. Even limited to one wildly out-of-focus eye, I could see I was in a world of hurt. Filthy, half-blind, and covered with charred clothing, I had no idea of where I was, who I was, or what had happened. I crawled out of the water and somehow stumbled into camp.

The fire ring was now a flat circle of shining black glass. The stately hemlock grove had been hosed down with a flamethrower. Brittle-dead ferns and rocks covered with brittle brown moss formed a larger circle beyond the blast radius. Blundering closer to the center of camp, I saw that the fire ring wasn't flat after all; there was a twisted log of strange grey wood half-buried in the center. Black glass snapped and cracked under the solidified remains of my boots as I stooped down and tugged it from the blasted earth. Cradling the salamander's cocoon in my arms, I stumbled and bumbled uphill and along the edge of the bluff until I found the spot where I had discovered it. I dumped it into the irregular crater and then turned to see the bright, clean sun peeping over the eastern lip of Peckerwood Canyon.

Then trees were rushing by overhead at a dizzying speed, and the head of a middle-aged man with a deeply weathered face and a week's worth of stubble loomed over me. A rushing wind tore at his words and my head felt stuffed with cotton, but I could lip-read what he was saying.

"You're all right. You're fine now, ole' boy. You just hang on and we'll get you fixed up."

Even with one half-ruined eye, I could see he didn't believe it himself. I looked to either side and saw I was in the rusty bed of a pickup, tucked between a couple of chainsaws and coils of steel cable.

I managed to croak out a single question and stay conscious long enough to get most of the answer.

"How'd you find me?"

He smiled to reveal a scattering of crooked teeth.

"We're cuttin' timber down on Pea Branch when you come out of the woods from upstream."He laughed. "Buford stepped away to take a leak when he seen you walkin' down the middle of the creek. You like scared the shit out of us! What happened to you son?"

Pea Branch? That was on the far southern edge of the Tallulah. The region was a checkerboard mix of private and federal forest land where they still took out a good deal of timber. I had come nearly twenty miles with no recollection of a single step of the journey. The trip would have been a brutal one-day hump in the best of health. I wondered how long I had been stumbling around in the woods. No more than two days, I decided. More than that and the pigs would have got me for sure.

My mind raced for a believable answer. The solution was obvious; I decided that no matter what, it would be the story I would stick to.

"My stove blew up in my face. White gas."

Country boy shook his head and I only got a few words before blacking out.

"Damn son, you lucky to be … "

I don't remember the helicopter ride to the UAB burn unit in Birmingham, but that's where I began to come around. They saved my life and treated me with touching kindness. They extracted melted eyeglasses out of my face and peeled burned rubber off the bottoms of my feet while a pretty nurse held my bandaged hands. I got my first whirlpool treatments as they pecked away at the dead tissue mixed with charred cotton. I was numb with the fog of morphine, and they didn't put sugar on anything. My right eye was kaput; my left would only provide a limited view of the world. My hands, face, chest, and lower legs would require a series of skin grafts. My lungs and trachea had been badly scorched, but seeing how it hadn't killed me outright, there was a good chance for recovery. A few people came to visit me but no one stayed long. I don't think they expected me to recover. I knew better. Even before I was transferred to Emory in Atlanta, the vision was beginning to come back in both eyes and

I hurt a little less every day.

The speed of my recovery at Emory turned me into a minor celebrity among the medical sect. My doctor was a tall drink of water who had earned her chops as an Air Force flight surgeon. She had seen more burned meat than a Texas steak house, and from the get-go, I could tell she didn't believe my story. I couldn't for the life of me figure out why, but she was constantly asking me about the incident — if I had remembered anything new or exactly where it had happened. I clung to my story and insisted the closest I could come to the spot where I had been blown up was the trailhead where my car had been parked. The woman came by at all hours to poke and prod and change the bandages herself. One morning she peered closely at my face and shook her head in disbelief. My eyebrows, hair, and whiskers were beginning to come back. The skin grafts were canceled; I didn't need them anymore.

The next day it was announced that there was no longer a reason to keep me. I was free to go out and hustle up eighty-nine grand to cover the tab. I had just put on my first real clothes in nearly a month when she came by to see me off. She waited until no one was in the room before she popped the question.

"So, tell me what really happened. I promise I won't make any moral judgments, but your burns were not from white gas or any other liquid fuel."

I shrugged in a noncommital way.

"I don't remember much."

She took my hands in hers, turning them this way and that, bending and peeking between the fingers and under the new nails. She looked into my eyes, and that's when I realized why I had gotten a little sweet on her. She was the carbon image of Old Cactus Girl, just cleaner, with fewer miles and decent makeup. I felt a pang of loss. Old Cactus Girl had been my favorite. I pretty much knew what had happened to me. I wondered what became of her.

"I know what happened out there in the woods. I've seen this several times before, you know."

I was doubtful. There was no way she could know unless I had talked while doped up with pain meds, and I knew damn well I hadn't. Even if I had blabbered the whole story, it would be considered the nonsense of a delirious condition.

"Oh yeah? Well, why don't you fill me in, doc?"

The doctor glanced around, then leaned in a little closer, boring into me with bright green eyes.

"No one knows where they're from or what they want. All we know is that they do terrible things to helpless people. That's all I can say and that's too much, but you deserve to know something. It's not your fault. We've never been able to find a pattern in the abductions. They happen at random. You're damn lucky they cut you loose like that logger up north. Most people never turn back up. We suspect their bodies are just dumped in deep space."

She smiled, and I couldn't get Old Cactus Girl out of my head.

"You must have been a real handful, Mr. Frances Flanagan."

"You have to be when you've got a girl's name. You know, sort of like a boy named Sue. Someone said they found a lot of dried blood in my ear canals when they first cleaned me up. Is that true?"

She chuckled and the green eyes sparkled.

"Yes, you had two ruptured eardrums, but at the time it was a low priority. They had healed by the time you arrived here. So, I guess whatever happened was pretty loud, huh?"

I smiled back, nodding stupidly with my very best deadpan expression. The more I was with her, the more I missed Old Cactus Girl, almost as much as I missed Pup. Well, if the woman wanted to believe that I had been scooped up and tortured by aliens, that was fine by me. Old Cactus Girl look-alike or not, I was ready to get my ass out of there. I stood to go and she pressed a card into my hands.

"After you've had some rest, you should go see him. Don't worry, he's an old friend and absolutely trustworthy. I work with him sometimes. In a … uh … case like yours, I think he would be willing to provide treatment pro bono."

It was a business card printed on thick stock with graceful cursive script announcing his specialty and Atlanta address on Peachtree Street.

Dr. Richard Solomon, MD, DPM.
Specializing in the treatment of
severe psychological and emotional trauma.

I could remember reading an article about him in a Sunday supplement. He was noted for groundbreaking treatment for folks who've had a harder time than most — the survivors of concentration camps, massacres, tornadoes, shipwrecks, and such. The article's author had neglected to mention he helped people recover from alien abduction. I thanked her, tucked the card into my flattened wallet, and stepped back into the outside world.

Passing the hat back at Emory had collected enough to pay for a one-way bus ticket back home. Back at work, they cut me loose, but tried to soften the blow by telling me the old near-lie: 'We'll call you when we need you.' Unemployment was barely enough to keep the lights on in the old wood frame house, not that I needed much now in the way of electricity. Sometime during my absence, thieves had taken everything but the refrigerator and the light bulbs. My car had ended up at the county impound lot where someone, obviously convinced I wasn't coming back, had stripped it of tires and rims. Disability might have been an option, except there was nothing wrong with me physically. No one seemed to care about the inside, and to be frank, that's the wider world's hard luck, or perhaps not. Even if I was believed, there wasn't anything anyone could do about what was coming.

It was a year to the day when I drove a borrowed car down to the Tallulah and hiked back to Peckerwood Canyon. I was almost hoping I couldn't find it, but after only three hours on the trail, I was standing at the entrance, still blocked by a massive plug of limestone woven together with centuries of trees and briars. This time I had plenty of daylight and some basic climbing equipment. I was repelling down the opposite side of the plug before lunchtime. The big woodpeckers were nowhere to be seen, but the canyon was just the same — the last true virgin backwoods in North Alabama, or North America for that matter.

I worked my way up the bubbling stream of clear water as darters and crayfish scuttled for cover. The spot where it had all happened was about as hard to find as the Trinity test site.

Brushing back a few limbs and fallen leaves, it was still a perfect circle of greenish-black glass about ten feet in diameter. There were a few scraps of dirty nylon with melted edges strewn around. The remains of my food bag still dangled from the limb where I had hung it that late afternoon. All the trees within the blast radius were clearly dead or dying.

It was still right where I had left it, the tip of one end poking up from the dry tan soil under the shadow of the bluff. There was no mistaking it for what it was: the incredibly fine grain, the odd color, the knots twisted into the scowling faces of pagan gods. I brushed away some of the soil surrounding it, then gave it a good tug. It refused to budge. I dug down a little deeper to quickly discover it was as deeply embedded in the living limestone as a dinosaur fossil. It had taken one year to migrate downwards through about eighteen inches of limestone. There was a familiar flap of wings behind me, and I turned to find one of the giant woodpeckers watching me from a nearby limb. It cut loose with its absurdly abrasive song, followed by a sudden silence. Cocking its head just so, we both listened to a chorus of replies from its own kind. It was time to go, but there were still a couple of things to do. I carefully covered the exposed end of the cocoon with a layer of soil, disguising my work with stones and fallen tree limbs. Then I made my way down to the blast ring and filled an empty coffee can with black sand. Then I left. I haven't been back to the Tallulah since.

It's easy to forget about in the daytime — that's when I can stay busy mowing yards when it's warm and raking yards or cleaning gutters when it's cold. It's the nights that are tough. Tough to fall asleep no matter how hard I've worked that day, and tough to face the dreams when I finally do drop off. I hear them singing in my dreams, and sometimes I can feel them shaking the earth right up to the frame of my bed. Although most are still many miles down, their million-year cycle of migration up from the molten iron-nickel core of the planet is as unstoppable as the solar wind. Ten years or a hundred years, next week or the next millennia, they'll be here in their own time, and time has no meaning to them. I don't know how many of them there are, or if they'll all show up at once or as individuals, but they'll be here.

Still written off as nothing more than a scientific curiosity, more and more tremors are disturbing the placid geology of North Alabama. Just powerful enough to muddy up a spring or crack the base of an old chimney. All I can do now is be patient and hope I live long enough to see the great migration surface.

Sometimes I look at the card I was given back at Emory, but I can't quite bring myself to call. I've certainly learned not to go backpacking alone. For now, especially at night, when a storm begins to roll in or the house shakes on its foundation for no reason, or the dreams are just too outrageous to ignore, I dig out the jar. Then I pour the musical black sand from one hand into the other until dawn, finding comfort in the distant echoes of the salamander's song.

THE END

GORT'S
BUTT

Gort's Butt

I'm too young to remember when the Neighbors threatened to kill us. Although there had always been a good deal of speculation, no one knew for sure if there was really anyone out there at all. President Truman plausibly claimed he didn't know. For once in his life, doddering old Joe Stalin professed believable innocence. My first-grade teacher, Mrs. Hardcastle, whom I adored and who seemed to know just about everything, was admittedly ignorant on the subject.

Our preacher, Brother Larimore, didn't know, didn't care, and eventually went to his death scoffing at the very possibility like some old sage who can't quite visualize the earth as anything but flat. True to our character, the overwhelming majority of Americans was also skeptical at first, saying it had to be some sort of commie trick, but they eventually came around. Exist they did, whether we believed it or not. When the Permanent Peace came knocking on the door, the time of mankind wallowing in gloriously innocent savagery was over, or it should have been.

That very first flying saucer came tearing in so fast that the most advanced radar in the world could only do a double take. When it finally did slow down, jaws hit control tower floors from London to Los Angeles. Nothing and no one could survive deceleration like that. Try slamming on the brakes with both feet at Mach 20 and you'll find out why. If a more effective way is known to turn a pilot inside out, I haven't heard about it. Anyone stupid enough to try such a maneuver would have to be scraped off the dashboard with a razor blade. When the alien saucer touched down on the National Mall in Washington, it had about as much impact as a toy balloon. It was an odd sort of reception: throngs of curious citizens mixed with an assortment of heavily armed troops and absolutely no one in charge, unless you counted the cops keeping people behind the white ropes. The visitor might as well have been Captain Cook landing on an island infested with cannibals.

He emerged and the cannibals gawked. Klaatu (a.k.a. Mr. Carpenter), man's <u>first</u> official ambassador from alien worlds, had arrived in peace, so we shot him.

The thing that's always puzzled me is that you well know that "they" have been watching us for ages. Anyone even halfway paying attention would have known that, if you came crashing in unannounced on planet Earth, it was liable to scare folks. They should have known that frightened people are dangerous people.

They should have known making a sudden move with a crowd of bewildered, armed-to-the-teeth, badly frightened humans was just begging for trouble. And that's exactly what they got. They always claimed it was nothing but a gift to help our president study life on other worlds, and I have no doubt that's true, but they should have picked one that didn't look like some kind of firearm. Down around here that's a good way to get you shot, and of course that's just what happened. At least Klaatu could have wrapped it in the Sunday funnies or put a bow on the damn thing or something.

Heck, I probably would have shot him myself. But I don't think I would have shot him a second time, not after an introduction to one of their all-powerful and immortal robots, the Gort. Even without the robots, a man who can travel between the stars like driving across town and self-resurrect when killed is nobody to mess around with.

We had to learn the hard way; by and large, that's human nature. And things are better now because of them. You look at the history tapes and see the carnage and squandered resources, and it's almost impossible to believe we used to live like that. Now people like to tell themselves we're all past that now, that even if they hadn't arrived when they did, we would have eventually sorted out all our troubles, but I doubt it. They laid down the law in no uncertain terms: end our old evil ways of blasting the hell out of each other or face wholesale extermination. It took some doing, but faced with the Gorts, humanity had little choice but to get along and go along.

Some things, like human nature, haven't changed at all, and that's a good thing as far as I'm concerned. I suppose I would be happy as a fireman or medic, but I like being a detective, especially seeing how I'm the only one in town. One thing I like about the job is that I get to meet a lot of people from all walks of life, but I had never even thought of meeting a Neighbor. The closest a plumber or taxi driver ever gets to a Neighbor is watching one on TV dress down the UN General Assembly, or one looking suspiciously at his plate during a state dinner. The odds of a Neighbor knocking on your door are about the same as winning the Mississippi sweepstakes, but people do win.

I knew who he was the second I laid eyes on him. They just have that certain look and bearing. Nice charcoal-colored suits but nothing extravagant, average height, weight, and haircut. Usually they appear to be Caucasian, but not always. The Neighbors stand out almost because they don't stand out. One thing's for sure: when one wants to have a chat, you damn well listen up. I knew why he was there before he said a word, or at least I thought I did; now I was under the floodlight and he would be asking the questions. There was nothing to do but brazen it out. At least they've learned to knock.

"Good morning, sir. Are you Mr. Law?"

I stood up and extended my hand. I think I was shaking a little. Not every day you shake hands with a man who can order the destruction of the world with a few words. Well, no matter how I felt about them, I was required to follow the law right down to the letter, provide anything they ask for without hesitation, and above all, be polite. "Yes, sir, I'm Detective Law, what can I do for you?" His hand was firm and warm; just an ordinary hand.

"My name is Mr. Planter. I represent the Permanent Peace, and I was wondering if I could have a few moments of your time."

"Of course. Sit down. My friends call me Dewy."

The only reaction to that was a brief curious smile. He didn't offer, 'Well, you can call me Sam,' or 'You can call me Bill.' He just sat down and looked around my office decorated with the usual macho southern man stuff. A good-sized deer head, a few picture frames full of local stone arrowheads, and Civil War-era mini balls. He lingered for a long time on a picture of my dad after Iwo Jima — only nineteen, but he looked like a wizened old man who had seen too much, hollow-eyed, half-starved, but still mighty happy to be among the living. Despite the fact that it was a Monday morning and both courtrooms were in use, it had gone quiet as Lincoln's tomb out in the hallway.

He took a deep breath through his nose and asked me the last thing I would have expected from a Neighbor.

"Detective Law …"

"Call me Dewy. I've never met a Neighbor before. This is a real honor."

"Thank you, although we prefer to be called Representatives. Dewy, what is that wonderful smell? Are you … cooking a meal?"

He said the phrase, 'cooking a meal' after a moment of hesitation; he had to stop and remember it. Like any decent investigator, I filed the fact away for later reference — the Neighbors don't do much cooking.

"No sir, I just got here a few minutes ago and put on a pot of coffee. Would you like a cup? It's Kenyan AA."

"I've read about coffee and I appreciate your offer, but I'm not allowed to sample mood-altering substances."

"The effects are very mild and quite enjoyable. I think your bosses mean heroin or moonshine, not coffee."

I could see he was curious; I picked out my best cup and topped it off for him. I suspected they had instructions to go along with the locals whenever possible. God, this was a fair way to see how far he would go to humor me. "Cream or sugar?"

"Sugar — I know what that is. What is cream?"

"It's made from milk, smooths out the bitterness; it's the way I drink mine."

He shifted a little uneasily in his chair. "Milk, you mean human milk?"

I laughed. "Lord no! Cow's milk. Gives you good strong bones. Here, just give it a sip; if you don't like it you sure don't have to drink it. What do you think we are? Savages? Go ahead and give it a try. The boss will let you drink milk, won't he?"

"Now that I've thought a little about it, don't you mix this with cow blood?"

I got a little annoyed with that, but at least it was something a little different. When you're from Alabama, you get a lot of unfunny crap. It ranges from the mildly offensive remarks about how we all marry our cousins to the truly obnoxious comments about cross-burning, lynchings, and such. I was firm but polite. I decided he might be lost.

"You're not visiting Masai tribesmen. That's in Africa. You're now located in New Garnett, Alabama. Mr. Planter, are you sure you're in the right place?"

"Oh, I'm quite sure."

To the man's credit, he took a tiny sip, then after a nod of approval, took another.

"Why, that's quite good. And that wonderful aroma. I think I also detect a mildly stimulating effect."

"That's the caffeine. Did you know the pyramids and the Great Wall of China were built without the first cup of coffee? Hell, I can't even get out of bed without the stuff. How on Earth can you folks get along without coffee?"

He pondered the question while taking another sip. "Why, Dewy, we're not usually on Earth."

He didn't laugh because he wasn't joking, but it was another tidbit. They don't spend much time here, and they just might have a quiet little sense of humor. I filled my own cup and commented on what a nice day it was, trying to feel him out. He asked about the mounted largemouth bass hanging on one wall, and I gave him a brief rundown on the sport of angling. He nodded politely, but I got the feeling I was bragging about my collection of scalps and shrunken heads.

After a few more pleasantries, he walked over to my window and gestured outside with his cup. "I see that your community has landscaped the area around the Gort. I've never seen that. None of us have. To be candid, most people try to hide them. Vegetation will be allowed to conceal them from view or something constructed around them."

"That's understandable. How would you like it if we parked a battleship on the lawn of your county courthouse?"

"We wouldn't like it, nor would we allow it, unless, of course, we agreed to it. So, why don't you conceal the Gort?"

"That's a fair question. Truth be told, when it first showed up, people were scared out of their socks. We thought it was here to wipe us out like the one that squashed that renegade Russian. Well, it just stood there like a junked car, and before you know, it was knee-deep in weeds. Then the blackberry and poison ivy grew all over it, and that kept folks from messing with it. In just a few years it was nothing but a patch of scrubby woods on the courthouse lawn. It went on like that for a good while until a young girl was playing nearby and got bit by a copperhead. She was in my sixth-grade class."

"Copperhead?"

"Yeah, it's a venomous snake. They did brief you about snakes, didn't they?"

Planter was the very picture of polite concern. "Of course. The young girl, did she die?"

"No, but she almost did. It made her mighty sick, and she lost her big toe. The next day her family showed up and cleared it all out. Didn't ask permission. Just went to work. They had some harsh words with the mayor over it, but the chief of police had better sense than to try and stop them. Then someone planted some flowers. Next thing you knew it had a little white picket fence. People stopped being scared and started taking a little pride in it. After all, not every town has its own Gort. You wouldn't know why your bosses put it here would you?"

He kept looking at the Gort, and I tried to remain calm.

"No one knows. We do not control the Gorts. They do as they will and we do our best to accommodate them. It is, however, a symbiotic relationship. Dewy, may I ask you a confidential question?"

I thought I was caught for sure. I stood by him and looked hard at the Gort, but I couldn't see anything incriminating. Gort's butt was tastefully concealed behind a camellia bush full of big red blooms. Did these jokers have X-ray vision? Didn't matter. All I could do now was take my medicine.

It had been a long time in coming — a good twenty years. I felt like I had caught my thumb with a treble hook.

"Sure, fire away."

"Why do people resent us?"

It was a strange question, but I was right proud to have it. I determined to pounce on it and steer it as far away from the Gort as possible.

"Why would we resent you? Look at all you did for us. There's no more war between nations, nobody goes hungry because there's no food. We don't waste all our money on weapons and pointless fights. We're healthier than at any time in history. Heck, I'm grateful you finally came along. We probably would have wiped ourselves out with atomic weapons if you hadn't."

"I'm given to understand that was considered a certainty. So tell me, if you can, why are we resented?"

I felt a bead of sweat pop out on my forehead. In an instant, he had gone from the innocent abroad to 'Berlin wants answers.' For the first time in my life, I felt a twinge of pity for all the thieves and cheats I've had under hot lights. I couldn't duck the question, so I tried to put the best face on it.

"There are some people who are ungrateful, but not many, just a tiny minority. You see them moaning, bitching every night on the news, but they'll never amount to much. Bellyachers never do."

"But why?"

"Various reasons. Even after what happened in Russia, some folks think you're in cahoots with the communists. It's tough to follow their line of reasoning, but they have a hard core of true believers. They talk big and tough, but one punch in the nose will shut 'em the hell up. Some think you work for the devil, but these are the same folks who think dinosaurs drowned in Noah's flood, so I wouldn't worry so much about them. Some radical politicians want to re-arm and kick you off the planet and out of our solar system. They're a small group, but you better watch 'em close. It's hard to tell if they really believe it or if they're just using that fear as a way to get elected. Still, I'd keep a close eye on them. There's a good many folks that think you're not doing anything at all for us. When that storm hit the coast last week, a lot of people were wondering out loud why you didn't help us stop it. Over in Russia, they're still mad about that Gort killing off half their army in thirty seconds."

"The Gort was provoked after repeated warnings."

"They thought you were bluffing."

"You're the only civilization to take that attitude in seven hundred and fifty-two local years. The last time a civilization initiated hostilities with a Gort, the aggressors were obliterated."

That really gave me pause; these people were willing to commit genocide to have it their way. That made them at least as bad as us. I topped his cup and decided to take the ball onto his side of the court.

"As long as we're on the subject of what happened to the Russians, can you tell me why the Gort stopped shooting?"

"That was the first and only time one did stop. It caused a good deal of distress in some circles when it failed to exterminate your civilization."

"I'm a bit distressed about it myself, but for different reasons. Most people assume you told it to stand down as they used to say. That we were special and you just couldn't bring yourselves to … uh — "

"Sterilize the threat? We had nothing to do with it. I don't think you understand, Dewy; we have no real control over the Gorts. No one was more surprised than the Permanent Peace when it stopped the destruction. Like I said, it's never happened before. Worlds have been destroyed with far less provocation. Only the Gorts know why you were spared, and they never said why."

"Why would you build a machine you couldn't control? Or that won't even communicate with you? That makes no sense."

"You seem like an honest man, Dewy, so I'll confide in you a little. We did not build the Gorts. We have no idea who did or when — only that they preserve the peace and protect countless worlds. Trillions of intelligent beings live peaceful, happy lives because of them. Do you mind if we go down to the Gort? I would like to take a closer look at it."

I forced myself to remain calm; you get a lot of practice at that in my line of work. He hadn't said a thing about the Gort's butt, but I knew they had to know. The courthouse had become almost completely deserted during the time Planter had been in my office. Blind Bill was still at the concession stand on the first floor sitting behind colorful ranks of candy and cigarettes. He nodded pleasantly when we walked past.

We went through the little picket fence and stood in front of the massive robot. The camellias had gotten pretty bushy. That gave me a slender thread of hope that he might not notice. Although it hadn't moved since that night, I've always been unable to shake the feeling that the robot recognized me whenever I came around, biding its time til it was ready to settle old scores.

Planter seemed completely at ease with the ten-foot-tall

doomsday machine, and after a few moments ran his hand across its dull silver torso and examined his fingertips. "It's got some sort of … material adhering to the surface."

I shrugged. "It's called tortoise wax. People usually put it on their cars to make them shine like new and protect the finish from the elements. Blind Bill gives it a good coat of wax every now and then and buffs it out. Shines like a new silver dollar when he's done."

"Who's Blind Bill?"

"He's the old Black gentleman who's got the refreshment stand on the first floor. Bill is blind as a sack of nails. Poor guy lost his vision when he was a kid. We said he got a hold of some bad moonshine. Look, Bill's a hell of a good guy; he'd give you the shirt off his back if you needed it. Please don't be hard on him. He wouldn't hurt a fly."

"Dewy, I've traveled extensively to inspect Gorts on many worlds, but this is the first time I've ever seen one cared for so lovingly, or even seen one cared for at all. There's one high in the Atlas Mountains that some locals found. Now every year there is an annual religious pilgrimage where thousands of people come just to throw rocks at it. People do it so much they have to dig it out just so they can do it all over again."

"Yeah, I heard of that. They call it the 'stoning of the new devil.' The authorities tried to put a stop to it, but all they accomplished was starting a riot. I can't see how a few rocks are going to damage one of the Gorts, or even leave a mark for that matter. Sorry, we're trying the best we can. Say, just out of curiosity, how many do you … uh … "they" ... usually station on a planet?"

"Until we contacted your civilization, there was never more than one attached to any one planet. Your world has nine that we are aware of. There may be more hidden in remote locations — on the sea floor or in active volcanoes."

"That's remarkable. Any idea why?"

"No, there is a good deal of speculation. I would really rather not elaborate."

He began to work his way around behind the robot, finally stopping to brush back the camellias for a good look at the machine's backside. He stared at it for what seemed like an eternity, then stepped back and motioned me closer. "Dewy, what are those words on the robot?"

"It's called graffiti."

"I know that. Can you read it aloud for me? I want to make sure I understand its meaning."

Now I was a bank robber who got himself locked in the vault or the guy who robbed a gas station and dropped his wallet on his way out the door. He knew damn well what it said, but for some reason, he wanted to hear me say it. After three decades the metal-flake purple was just as vivid as the day it had come out of the can. "It says, GORT'S BUTT!"

"The smaller letters, what do they say?"

"Go Bulldogs."

"Why? I don't understand. I don't understand. It's impossible."

"It was just some kids out on a lark with a couple of cans of spray paint. We've tried everything to get it off — solvents, sandblasting, blowtorch, you name it — but nothing ever worked. If you have something we can use, we'll be happy to try it out."

He shook his head and sat down on the little iron bench the New Garnett Ladies' Flower and Garden Club donated last year. "Dewy, do you know what we call your planet? Not officially, but in casual conversations."

"No, but it's probably not very flattering."

"We call Earth 'the impossible world.'"

"The impossible world? Why?"

"Because that's what it is. Observe the current weather conditions."

"Nothing to complain about there. Flowers are blooming, grass is starting to green up, the birds are singing. It's a wonderful spring day."

"What about last week? That wasn't so wonderful was it?"

"No, nothing wonderful about a hurricane hitting New Orleans. At least it doesn't happen every day."

"That's my point. Look, last week this region of Earth was hit by terribly destructive storms. A fair number of people died or were injured, and thousands of homes were obliterated in the span of only a few hours. Even this far inland you were flooded by torrential rains. Today it is very pleasant, but soon it will become unbearably hot. Before the year is out, it will become cold enough to turn water into a solid. This is the only world known where such radical environmental changes happen with such regularity. In addition, you endure active volcanos, seismic hyperactivity, and the occasional hit from an asteroid or comet."

I failed to see his point. "So what, we're not the only danger spot in the galaxy."

"The list of hazards on Earth is endless. It's questionable that life would even become established in such a violent world. Yet it has and life thrives. Life on planet Earth has tenacity unmatched anywhere else in the known universe. It not only thrives ... it's ... it's ... comfortable. Are you aware there is a carnivore sleeping in the middle of your main street?"

Alarmed, I jumped up and rushed to my window, which afforded me a view of the business district. I expected an audacious coyote or maybe even a disoriented bobcat, but all I saw was Bulger. "You mean the dog? Oh, that's just Bulger; you might call him the town watchdog. He's getting on in years. I think the warm pavement feels good on his bones."

"I observed this canine for a substantial length of time. It's right in the middle of the street, but people maneuver their vehicles around the sleeping animal."

I whistled and Bulger ignored me. "Ah, traffic's slow today. He's all right. If anyone hurt the old yeller hound, I'd have to lock them up for their own protection."

"But this is a planet red in tooth and claw. Or at least that's what we were briefed."

"Sometimes it is, but not always. Hey, we're just used to it. You can get used to anything. I mean, it might be a chore, but it's not impossible to live here."

"But it should be! Just like the graffiti on the robot's posterior. The Gorts cannot be harmed with any weapon known. A Gort can pass through the heart of a star without damage. They are immortal and unchanging. No known substance will adhere to the surface of one, yet it has some sort of message painted on its backside, plus a coat of protective wax."

For better or worse, one thing the Permanent Peace did improve was communications — radios never lose a signal, and even static is a thing of the past. The Permanent Peace can be a pain in the neck, so when I got buzzed, it was a relief. It was a convenient excuse to end the interview. I was hoping he had found whatever the hell he had come to find and would quietly depart New Garnett forever. Even when it was a report of two needless deaths, I wasn't exactly disappointed. I closed the link and tried to sound official and important. "Sorry, Mr. Planter, I've got to go work a crime scene. You're welcome to drop by my office anytime in the future if you think I can be of any more assistance."

"Is it an emergency?"

"Not anymore. Sounds like a couple of tough guys fought a duel down at River Walk Park last night and they both lost. Some lady walking her dog found them a while ago. There's nothing I can do about it now but write a report and notify the families, but I have to go check it out first. Sometimes it's just a cold-blooded murder made to look like a duel, as if that would make a difference. Either way, it's an unjustified killing."

He didn't miss a beat or show a molecule of surprise.

"A duel, that's a form of ritualized combat, isn't it?"

"Yeah, but it doesn't matter how ritualized it was. It's still murder. Sorry, got to saddle up. Nice meeting you."

"Do you mind if I go with you? I will not interfere in any way."

Hell yes, I minded, but I didn't let on that I did. "Mr. Planter, federal, state, and local law say I have to cooperate with any request you make as long as no one is harmed or endangered. I think you ought to know it's going to be ugly and messy. Once you see it, you won't be able to not see it. It's liable to ruin your appetite at the very least. I know it ruins mine, and I've seen it more times than I can count."

"I assure you I will be fine. I do appreciate your consideration. Shall we go?"

We walked across the street to my pickup truck. Even though the visor remained down I could feel the Gort watching us until we were out of sight.

One duelist lay face down on the short grass. Hit in the face, the back of his head resembled a watermelon mauled by a hungry coyote. Dried brain tissue mixed with dog poop and cigarette butts formed a faint halo around the deceased. Sitting on the concrete bench of a nearby picnic table was his opponent, frozen by rigor mortis with the old cap-and-ball pistol gripped tightly in his dead hand. His head had frozen into an unfeasible position. Struck dead in the Adam's apple, the bullet and hydrostatic shock turned muscle and bone into gel, and gently laid his face flat on top of his right shoulder. Their blood had blended and dried like any liquid and had drained toward the river, seeking out the Gulf of Mexico, five hundred miles away.

The medics had done me the courtesy of leaving the bodies exposed to the sky and the flies. It was pretty cut and dried as far as I could tell. I've seen sudden death more than rainy days — that comes with the job, but this is always sickening. It's always tough to see someone killed in a storm or car accident, but after all, when the good Lord says your time is up, your time is up. What these men did was just plain stupid. I actually felt a little embarrassed. I glanced back at Planter, half expecting to see him tossing his cookies into the nearest trash can. I was mildly surprised and impressed to see him only a few feet away, watching everything we did with an impassive interest. I discovered long ago there are two kinds of people in a situation like this: those who can't bear to look and those who can't turn away. Planter had not turned away at the sight of sudden needless death, but he wasn't wrapped in morbid fascination either. He processed a detached clinical pity, like he felt sorry for the victims but was only willing to expend a preset amount of sympathy on them. I pried the pistol away from the upright corpse and swung the cylinder out to make it safe. There had been a single round in the chamber. I checked the other man's weapon and found he had hedged his bets a little: he had loaded two rounds. Not very sporting, but he had only fired once.

"Are they known to you?"

"Nope, willing to bet you a bag of peanuts they're from another area."

I pulled on a pair of latex gloves and patted down the upright body. He didn't have much — a set of car keys and a wallet containing six dollars plus an Indiana driver's license. The laminated plastic was slick with gooey half-dried blood, and I held it up for Planter to examine. The man had been old enough to know better and was required to wear corrective lenses while driving.

"They're both Yanks, from up north; they came a good ways to do this. The Alabama legislature passed another really stupid law last year legalizing dueling between consenting adults. The Supreme Court overturned it, but people still come down south to do it."

"That is unfortunate. Why do you think they did it?"

I shrugged. "It's almost always over women, and occasionally it's about money, but not near as often. Men will kill each other over a woman quicker than anything else. I hope she didn't care for either one of these. But … but somebody cared for them, parents or siblings or even a spouse. It's a damn shame. On top of that, I've got to track down the next of kin. These idiots broke someone's heart and left it to a stranger to break the news."

He shook his head like I had gotten the answer wrong. "That is totally illogical. There is an abundance of reproductive-age females on Earth."

"Yeah, but looks like they were both sweet on the same one. Tell you something else, both these boys had seconds. They sure as hell didn't walk all the way here from Indiana. When the duelists killed each other, the seconds panicked, hopped in their cars, and got the hell out. They probably didn't let off the gas until they reached home. They forgot one of their flashlights. Judging from the looks of things, I'd say it happened about three or so this morning."

"Seconds? Is there some sort of manipulation of time involved?"

Another note into the file: the Neighbors may be able to monkey around with the flow of time. "No sir, a second in this situation is a trusted friend who keeps the proceedings honest. Both men bring someone who makes sure the other guy doesn't cheat. If someone tries to backshoot his opponent, his second heads him off, shouts a warning, or even shoots the malefactor himself. One of them did a right half-assed job and let the other guys go at it with two shots in the chamber. Or the man's second looked the other way for reasons of his own. Won't know until I find them and do a few interviews. The truth will come out. It always does. The bottom line is this is still a double murder with at least two accessories. There's a whole formal code of behavior associated with this, although that doesn't mean everyone fights fair."

I took some notes and photos, then waved the boys over with the meat wagon. Both duelists were zipped up and on their way to the county morgue inside of ten minutes. I heard a deep rumble off to the west and could see towering thunderheads peeping over the horizon. Planter watched the storm roll in while I wrote up the initial report. In a few minutes, it was already displaying dark sheets of rain laced with fingers of electricity. I finished up about the time the first real push of wind from the approaching thunderstorm washed over us. "Best get back to the barn. You don't want to be near water when the lightning starts to hit."

I could see he wanted to remain a little longer but had enough sense to defer to local expertise. I offered to buy him lunch, but not surprisingly, he politely declined. He didn't say much on the way back, and that was understandable. By now I had determined he was on his first real mission, and no amount of training can prepare anyone for the sight of real blood and guts.

We pulled into my parking slot just as fat drops of rain began to streak the windshield. "Sorry if that spoiled your appetite, but to tell the truth, I only took you along with me because I had to."

I was expecting a lecture on how we were hopelessly violent barbarians, but that's not what I got. "It was not your fault, Dewy; to the contrary, I believe you would have attempted to stop them even at risk to your own life. Isn't that correct?"

"I suppose so. I'm just embarrassed more than anything. Mr. Planter, we're not all bloodthirsty savages. We've got a lot of good people who abhor violence. It's not always blood and thunder down here, you know. Tell you what, when the weather cools down this fall, I'll take you out to the woods. Tallulah National Wilderness is just an hour's drive away and it's drop-dead gorgeous when the leaves turn. The snakes will be hibernating, no bugs or poison ivy; it's the best time to go. We'll go get lost in the sticks for a few days."

I could see the wheels turning. Another penetrating observation percolated to the surface.

"I was given to understand a wilderness was an unpopulated

area, like Antarctica or Siberia."

"Well sure, but we keep what we can in a natural state, someplace folks can camp and hunt and go skinny-dipping. There's more to life than just a paycheck, you know."

This seemed to please him immensely. "Thank you, Dewy, that's just the kind of thing that's been so difficult for us to access and understand. I think you have done more to enlighten us in a single day than your world's leaders have in thirty years. I want you to take this as a token of our friendship and high esteem."

He handed over an object the size of a playing card and the thickness of an old quarter. Aside from a small hole in one corner, the diameter of a number two pencil, it was featureless. Smooth as glass and warm to the touch, it appeared to be made from the same stuff as their robots and spaceships. Planter instructed me on its use before I could ask what it was. His voice took another shift up the scale in authority. This wasn't a cheap bauble to impress the savage, and I was being trusted with something of importance. I was a long way from sure that I wanted anything from him. What followed had an eerie similarity to a brief lecture on firearms safety before being handed a loaded machine gun.

"Keep it on your person at all times. You are now officially a native consultant of the Permanent Peace and therefore under our protection. Refer to it in an emergency or anytime you feel your safety is in jeopardy. I must go now, but I'll be in contact soon. Remember, always keep it within arm's reach. There aren't very many of these, and if even one is lost, it is likely there won't be any replacements. Good day, Dewy. I'll be in touch very soon."

Without another word, he got out of the pickup and began to walk down a nearly deserted Main Street. I studied the silver card for a few seconds, looking for a button or switch before giving up. How I was supposed to make a call with it was beyond me. What was I supposed to do with this if I got in a jam, throw it at … throw it at whom? When I looked up, Planter was gone.

That, as they say, had been a close shave. If he suspected the truth about Gort's butt, he didn't let on, but the Neighbors have a poker face that would have put Wild Bill Hickok to shame. Try listening to one of the old newsreels of Carpenter delivering the ultimatum after his resurrection. He's no more upset than someone dressing down the paperboy for missing too many deliveries. Little wonder that most people thought he was bullshitting, a dirty commie trick. That attitude was wiped away along with the Third Soviet Shock Army on May the first in the year of our Lord 1950. A single Gort had annihilated an army of over one hundred thousand strong in less time that it takes to change a light bulb. As far as I knew, it could have been done by the same machine that stood on the courthouse lawn.

But like I had told Planter, it's not possible to live in fear forever. Sooner or later people just lose their fear, or the threat is replaced by a danger more pressing, like copperhead snakes and poison oak. It was the New Garnett Ladies' Flower and Garden Club that installed the little white picket fence around the Gort after the area had been cleaned up. Over the years they added camellias and azaleas bordered with a bright carpet of pansies and such. The authorities never objected. The authorities tried to pretend the Gorts didn't even exist. What they did mind was the other things people did with the Gort.

It started simply enough. A red felt Santa hat, the kind with the little white ball on the end, and a white fake fur band was covering Gort's head on Christmas morning, 1955. It must have taken a trainload of guts to prop a ladder against the robot in the freezing-ass, cold dead of night and plant a Santa hat on the assassin of worlds, but done it someone had. The culprits were never caught. For a while, the Gort was kept under heavy guard, which was removed when things cooled down a bit. Dawn on the following Easter morning found the robot sporting a pair of floppy pink ears wired to its chinless head. The same routine followed: outraged city fathers and scowling federal officials demanded the persons responsible, with the exact same results. The culprits were never identified, things cooled down, and the state troopers withdrew to more pressing duties. A tradition had been born.

Dawn, on the following Fourth of July, had found the robot in the guise of Uncle Sam. It actually had a bit of charm as old Sam — a fake cotton beard wired to a star-spangled paper mache hat that came down to his visor. The pranksters had somehow stuck a tiny flag into one massive metal fist. By now it had become a rite of passage for the more adventurous young people who dreamed up ever more elaborate costumes. The more times it happened, the more muted the official response became. Finally, although the federals didn't actually come out and say so, the implied position was that only an idiot would mess with a Gort, but as long as it didn't react, there was probably no harm done. Gort's costumes became more elaborate by the year: Gort the leprechaun, Gort the groundhog, and Gort the Thanksgiving pilgrim. By the time I was a senior in high school, people said it had all been done, but to me that was an obvious lie. I had thought of something that hadn't been done. It hadn't been attempted because everyone had assumed it was impossible. But like they say, you never know until you try.

My turn to try came when I was a high school senior, on a cool October night the weekend before homecoming. The New Garnett Bulldogs were slated to take on the Rockport Raiders, a notoriously ferocious team from the blackbelt country of South Alabama. In those days the Raiders consistently whipped their opponents like hapless galley slaves. Homecoming games are traditionally played against inferior teams or at least ones you have a fighting chance of besting, but some idiot had scheduled a homecoming against Rockport. Not only were they superb players by anyone's measure, but also they were mostly Black farm boys who spent summers tossing bales of hay onto flatbed trucks and driving fence posts by hand. The Raiders had only been playing all-white teams for a few seasons and they never, ever, lost. It was generally agreed that whoever had scheduled the Raiders as a homecoming opponent was either a traitor or an imbecile, but there it was, and there was no backing out.

I don't even remember who I went camping with that night. Bob Cranshaw for sure. We had gone in his vehicle, an ancient wood-paneled station wagon we affectionately called the barf barge. Bob had given a mere seventy-five bucks for the barge before discovering that a long-forgotten passenger had somehow managed to puke into the defrost vent. The defroster leaked the faint odor of stale vomit every time it was switched on, but the wagon was rugged enough to shrug off abuse from a gang of high school boys, and it was easy to service under backyard shade trees. It suited us all fine. We just tried to avoid using the defroster whenever possible. That fateful Saturday night we jammed into the barge and headed for Spanish Fields, a rough patch of ground, part free shooting range, part open campground, part town dump. Today it's a sanitized kiddie park.

Hernando De Soto and his band of cutthroats had wintered on the same spot four hundred years before by the shores of the ill-tempered Tennessee River. Local legend had it that the first European settlers discovered some relics from the doomed Spanish expedition, and there was a fortune in Inca gold buried on the site, just waiting to be found. There had been a stockade built there by settlers and burned during the War of the Red Sticks, with a great loss of life on both sides. New Garnett's military contribution to The Mexican-American War and the War Between the States had been formed and trained on the same grounds. Boys from New Garnett and Tallulah County had reported here in 1898, 1917 and late 1941. There had been plans to turn the area into a formal base for National Guard and Reserve troops, but the Neighbors had made the military obsolete. The old stomping ground of Spanish conquistadores and ferocious Confederate fighting men became a place for high school kids to drink beer and go parking with their dates.

We squatted around the bonfire drinking Dixie Star beer and gagged on Sphinx cigarettes, swapped absolute truths with bald-faced lies with the skill of professional diplomats. We talked about girls endlessly, a subject of which, in retrospect, we were shockingly ignorant, but we knew who we liked and why. Some things were universally agreed upon: who had the best-looking bottom in New Garnett High School? Little Annie Lee Loveless, that's who! Some things were the source of endless and pointless disagreements: could the Rockport Raiders be decisively defeated by the New Garnett Bulldogs? Is it true the weather lady on Channel 2 got busted once for prostitution? Finally, the open question I had been waiting for arrived: is the Gort on the courthouse lawn really an immortal destroyer of worlds or is it just a big fake to keep the local barbarians in line?

By the time my cue came up, we were all pretty well lubed, but not quite drunk enough to keep us safely by the fireside. I had been planning this for a long time, and I seized the moment with relish.

I kicked off with how ashamed I was that our loss to Rockport was a foregone conclusion. My buddies hung their heads in drunken shame, and a few muttered lame excuses about the opposition's superior athletic ability, coupled with a year-round training regimen that would make a Spartan beg for mercy. And with an opportunity to avenge themselves for past abuses, real and imagined. Plus, blessed with a talented coach, the Raiders were unbeatable.

Pure baloney, says I, you're never beaten until you admit you're beaten. What we had to do was something so radical, so outlandishly unachievable, it would begin to prey on the opposition's minds the second they heard about it.

Larry asked, "Just what the Sam Hill you propose to do, kidnap the robot and hold him hostage?"

I shook my head. "Nope, even if it were possible, that would bring nothing but trouble. We'd be found out like any other kidnappers. Besides, even if we could move the damn thing, there's no way we can cram a ten-foot-tall metal giant into the barf barge. No way we can tie it to the luggage rack. No telling what the son of a bitch weighs. It's got to be something simple but breathtakingly bold."

Reaching into my pack I pulled out my secret weapon and held it up in the firelight — a nearly full can of Testbed brand Number Six gloss, metal-flake purple spray paint. Then I made the announcement that I had been rehearsing for a month. "We're going to paint Gort's ass."

No one said anything; they all just stared at me in silent, wide-eyed horror. It was Larry who broke the silence by opening another can of Dixie with a church key. He took a deep slurp of warm suds before he finally spoke in that slow back-country drawl of his. "You're full of mud, Dewy. It's one thing to put a funny hat on the Gort but … you know damn well that the robot … well, you can't paint it because nothing will stick to it."

I was ready for that. "Oh yeah? Blind Bill puts a coat of car wax on it every few months. If car wax sticks to the Gort, other things will stick to it too." I shook the can like a medicine man's sacred rattle. "This shit will stick to the back of a greased coot! If you don't believe me, ask my mom about it! I got some on a pair of jeans and she like to go nuts over it. She threatened to stripe my big ass with a switch if I ever did it again."

Larry gestured toward the distant lights of New Garnett with his can of beer. "Chief Morgan catches us he'll do a lot more than that. Dewy, we all know you got a lot of sand in your craw, but that's just crazy. What if you set it off? Don't you recall what happened in Russia to Marshall what's-his-name?"

"How do you know it really happened? I think the whole thing was a put-up. You think the Ruskies would lie down and play dead if that really happened? Hell, Larry, they would fight it right down to the last man."

Larry shrugged. "I don't know Dewy, sounds awfully risky."

I was ready for that too. I unloaded on them like a war chief of old. "I cannot believe this shit! Desoto camped on this very same spot. They were sick and out of supplies, but do you think for one second he ever thought of turning back? Hell no! Bedford Forrest assembled right here before the battle of Mud Creek! They were outnumbered ten to one by people who would have them dancing on thin air if they got captured. They went on to beat the Yanks like they were dirty old rugs — the last major victory won by the Old Confederacy!"

I threw in a large dose of sarcasm. "Can you imagine Colonel Gurley coming up to General Nathan Bedford Forest and saying, 'Sorry, General Forest, that just sounds a little too scary to the boys. We all done decided it was best if we all just go home and slop the pigs.' They are watching us right now, boys! The whole lot of them: Desoto, Forrest, Weatherford, and Old Hickory! I'll go alone if I have to. I might get caught. Hell, I might get disappeared, but I'll never shame the heroic blood that runs in our veins!"

Bob was and still is a practical man with little patience for such nonsense. He's never been very athletic, but he more than makes up for it with a calm, analytical mind. "All right Dewy, let's suppose for a minute that that shit will stick to the Gort. Just how do you propose to get in there and get out without getting nabbed by Chief Morgan? He'll spot the barge for sure and he's not stupid. He'll put two and two together."

I decided I could stand one more Dixie. That's the devilish thing about Dixie Star — the first one tastes green as liquid smoke, and by the time you pop open the fourth, it goes down smooth as sweet iced tea. "The same way everyone else has gotten in and out. There's the entrance to a service tunnel in the old coal yard by the train tracks. They used the tunnel to move coal into town when they still heated everything with it. It's all grown up now, but it's still there. It runs all the way to town. There's an exit in an alley just two blocks from the robot. Bob stays in the old coal yard with the barge, and the rest of you come along to stand watch. I'll do the job and we get the hell out. We'll be back here in less than two hours, drinking Dixies."

Larry nodded, finished his brew, and tossed it into the blaze where the printing peeled as the steel began to glow like a hot cherry. "I never heard of a damn tunnel. How do you know it's there?"

I smiled. "Red Tuttle told me about it last year. He's been dating my oldest sister, and he bragged to me about the time they dressed Gort as a Thanksgiving pilgrim. I went down there myself to check it out last week. It runs for a good two miles and ends near the courthouse. It's dark, wet, and a little scary, but it's there just like Red said. Look, fellas, if it sounds a little too hairy, I'll go myself. Bob, would you ride me over there and wait for me?"

Bob didn't miss a beat; you could have been asking him for a ride to the bait store. "Sure thing, Dewy. What's the plan?"

Good old Bob, the man was always game, but when your car smells like puke whenever you run the heater or defroster, that's a good quality to have. "Simple as falling off a rotten log. Bob rides us over to the coal yard, stashes the wagon behind the old offices, and waits for us. Larry, you and Ronnie come with me through the tunnel to stand watch while I do the job."

I pulled out a pair of extra flashlights. "You fellas see Chief Morgan or any other trouble coming, give me one blink with the light. When it's all clear, give me two short blinks. We'll toss the empty can down in the coal tunnel and get the hell out. Then we spend the rest of the night in delicious anticipation of the discovery of our handiwork. But there's one thing you got to remember fellas, nobody brags, and nobody rats. We get caught, it'll be our asses for sure. I even got some camouflage to wear."

I hauled out my Dad's old fatigue jacket; he had worn it on both Iwo and Okinawa and given it to me when I was six. It was faded and threadbare, but since childhood, I had ascribed to it almost mystical properties of invisibility. "This was my Dad's lucky jacket. He wore it all through the war and never even stubbed his toe."

Larry raised a hand. "How come Red didn't keep his mouth shut?"

I explained. "A few months back I caught him and my sister making out on the back porch. He was already on second, getting ready to steal third, when I ruined everything. I had always suspected him in the Thanksgiving job, and I took him to task on it. I'm too big and strong to threaten, so we made a deal in exchange for my silence. He clued me in on the tunnel. It's nearly midnight, boys, we going or not?"

Keller Coal Company was already well on the way to extinction when the Neighbors landed. The Tennessee Valley Authority (TVA) had made it cheaper to heat with electricity, and all new locomotives ran on diesel. When the new power plants came online, coal was as obsolete as whale oil. It had all happened so fast that current stockpiles were abandoned along with uncounted mining operations. The last delivery never made it to the furnaces. All that remained of Keller Coal was a mountain range of soft, dirty, and worthless rocks dumped at the end of an unused rail spur. Every now and then there were rumors that someone was going to buy the property, but nothing ever came of it. It had sat undisturbed so long that sizable trees were already gaining a foothold, and a thin layer of new soil was inching up the slopes.

I plunged into a black gully, and the boys were right behind me. Making our way between peaks of crumbling bituminous coal, our flashlights shadow-boxed with light-absorbing slopes. In the dark, it was a monotonous landscape with only a few weeds for landmarks. I was almost getting worried when my light caught the flash of flaking chrome. Seconds later, a rounded metal hulk loomed out of the darkness. The tunnel's guardian was a rotting ten-ton dump truck crouching on flat tires above the overgrown entrance. Still, unless you knew exactly where, you would likely not find it, even at high noon. But it was there, a blacker hole in the blackness, veiled by a tangle of blackberry vines that were patiently tearing down a wooden door that had been pressed into service as a sign, and nailed to a sagging wooden utility pole. The words were thin, colorless shadows on the warped wood. They were missing a few members, but the meaning was still crystal clear. DANG R. In smaller letters below 'dang r' was the traditional 'o trespassi.'

Ron studied the words. "I think it says 'danger and no trespassing.'" He nodded in satisfaction like he had solved some byzantine grammatical puzzle. "Yep, that's it. 'Danger no trespassing.' I don't know, Dewy. Looks awful snaky."

I spoke in my most reassuring tone. "No problem. Too cold for snakes to be moving around."

Larry shook his head. "You mean we got to crawl through that? Damn Dewy, that's not a tunnel. That's a groundhog burrow."

That was the thing that always mystified me about the boy: how could someone so reckless with his liver be so timid about a little real adventure? I affected a nonchalant courage, but the entrance did in fact look a little smaller than when I had scouted it out. One thing for sure, if I was going to get help from them, I would have to get them really committed. "It's not a ride at the state fair, Larry, but it gets us to where we want to go. Right, Ronnie?"

Ronnie was silent, quickly looking from Larry back to me, trying to decide if this was worth all the effort. "Dewy, looks awfully muddy and dark. You been in there?"

I lied. "Yes, Tinkerbell, I been in there, for crying out loud. Boys, you want to be chickens about it, that's your business. Go on back to the barf barge and wait if you want. Me, I got a job to do."

With that, I switched on the flashlight, got down on all fours, and scrambled through the entrance. It was muddy and it was dark, but after a few feet past the thorny blackberry, it opened up into a wide cement tunnel topped by a roof of the same material. Clusters of stumpy pale stalactites clung to the ceiling like skeletal fingers dripping mineral-rich water. My light shone on a blocky bin of glistening wet coal just in front of me. I peered closer and saw wheels on the bottom of the bin, now welded by rust to a pair of narrow gauge rails.

Then Larry was through and standing behind me. "So this is the famous dang r o trespassi mine. What is that, Dewy? They got a train down here?"

I nodded like I knew what I was talking about. "Sure, that's how they used to get the coal into town. Looks like old Keller just walked off and left it." I pointed to the crumbling sides of the mine car — uniform heaps of coal lay where they had burst through the massive wooden planks. There were piles of moldering wooden boxes and the soft outlines of old tools mummified by a thick wrapping of corrosion. "In another ten or twenty years, it'll just be a long pile of coal. There's still plenty of room to squeeze by though."

Larry began to sidle between the train and the wall. Small avalanches of coal followed after him until he reached the front car and stood in the open tunnel, shining his light on the walls and ceiling.

Ronnie came in grunting through the low entrance and started laughing when he spotted the miniature train. Most of Ronnie's basement had been given over to his entire family's strange obsession: miniature trains. It was like a Lilliputian race of plastic people had colonized their basement and incorporated every square inch of room into their subterranean outpost. Tiny trains zoomed between perfect trees, through a scaled-down land of manicured farms and idealistic little towns populated with plastic, thimble-sized people and animals. We found Ronnie's hobby hokey beyond belief, but somehow oddly endearing.

The more Ronnie investigated the midget railway, the more enthusiastic he became. "Hot dog, would you look at this! This is just amazing! I never even thought of something like this." He got down on one knee and tapped a strip of ruined iron."Look at that dinky little gauge! They've got bigger rails than that on the kiddie train down at the duck park." He noticed Larry standing at the front of the train with his eyes cast down at something unseen. "Hey, Larry! Is there a tiny locomotive up front? Now that's something I'd like to have in the backyard."

Larry shook his head and motioned us forward. "I don't think you want this in your backyard, Ron."

Three lights played across a heap of rotting leather and coal-blackened bones. Scraps of hairless horsehide still clung to the ribs, and a grimy elongated skull lay on the ground with a single perfect puncture right between the eye sockets. Its thick teeth grinned back at us like we were all the butt of some unspeakably cruel and tasteless joke. Larry kneeled down and ran his fingers along the bones to the disintegrating collar drooped across the animal's carcass. A tangle of rotten leather and rusting chains bound the body to the lead coal car.

It was a horse. It looked like old man Keller just shot it and walked off. I've heard of things like that happening when the Permanent Peace set up shop. Keller got up one morning and no one wanted Keller coal anymore. It was hearsay they were getting ready to replace gasoline soon. Cars and trucks would run on those black power cubes like the electrical grid does now. Only they'd be small enough and cheap enough to put under the hood.

Ronnie had a good heart, he always hated to believe in the craven things desperate people would do, and he refused to believe this. "No way, that's worse than shooting you …"

The words hung in his mouth. I knew he wanted to recall what he had said the instant it came out. A silence cold enough to freeze the dripping water descended around us. I know he didn't mean to hurt me. Sometimes people hurt one another intentionally, sometimes with neglect, but I knew this had been purely by accident. Clenching my jaws hard enough to chip a tooth, I forced down the anger. By that point in my life, I had had a lot of practice. I had been known to pounce on other boys for far, far less.

I flashed the light from the slain horse's remains to Ron's face; he chose his words slowly and with care. "Oh my God, Dewy, I'm sorry, I'm so sorry. I didn't mean anything by that."

I squeezed my eyes tight enough to pop them from the sockets, but the tears still seeped through. I think that made me angrier than what Ron had said. "Not your fault man. Daddy didn't kill himself, boys. That little yellow-bellied asshole Tojo killed him. It just took a little longer."

I didn't even realize I had gotten nose to nose with poor Ron until Larry got between us, gently took me by the arm and began to move me back a little. "You know he didn't mean anything, Dewy. It's all right, buddy, they strung Tojo up and now he's roasting in hell where he belongs."

I hung my head and began to quietly snivel while my friends stood in mortified silence. Finally, I regained enough equilibrium to speak. "You're right, boys; it's a shame they couldn't execute the little backstabbing bastard more than once. You know, I never told anyone this, but Mom, when she's in her … in her cups … she don't blame the Japs. She blames the Neighbors."

They just looked at each other. Larry put an arm around my shoulder while Ron patted me on the back. "The Neighbors? Why, Dewy?"

"If they had arrived in time to stop the war from happening, Dad would still be alive. He wouldn't have had to go through all that … all the stuff he had to do to stay alive. Mom says millions of people died while the Neighbors just sat out there and watched it all happen. If the Nazis and Tojo had won, it would have been all the same to them — six of one and half a dozen of the other. She says the only reason they did anything was because we had the bomb and now we don't even have that. She's really bitter at 'em, boys."

Ronnie looked at me with big sorrowful eyes. "I didn't know your mom drank."

Larry punched Ronnie in the arm with enough force to leave a respectable bruise. "With you for a kid, Ronnie, I'm surprised your mom doesn't run her own still."

I squared my shoulders and hefted the old rucksack. "Come on, boys, we got us a mission."

The tunnel was as straight as a Jehovah's Witness. We walked for a couple of hundred yards before anyone spoke. Larry walked over to a mostly clean section of the wall and tapped the grimy cement. "Look, you can still see the grain from the wooden forms. They must have just dug a glorified ditch, poured the concrete, and covered her up."

Picking up a small iron spike that had worked its way from the rail bed, he struck the wall with a sharp metallic tone. The sound flowed down into the blackness and echoed away.

"We still got a good ways to go, boys. Larry, I know it looks solid, but let's not push our luck."

After another ten minutes, we spotted a sagging steel ladder propped against the wall. We followed the rungs upward with our lights and spotted a big circle of diamond steel plate, just in time to hear something like a muted jet roar past overhead. We instinctively ducked as tiny flakes of rust rained down like gritty brown sleet. I stood up and looked closely at the iron plate. "Looks like we're under Wheeler Road. That means we're over halfway there."

Larry pointed to the rim of the steel where it met the casing around the manhole. He pointed to a thin bead of rippling metal. "They welded the bastard shut. I'd hate to get all the way to the end just to find a locked door. Are you sure this is how they got at the robot?"

I didn't give the germ of doubt a chance to grow. "Sure I'm sure. It's how people have been getting at it all these years. It's been passed from senior class to senior class for decades. I just got in on the secret a little early, that's all. Even if it's welded, so what? It's just a bead of alloy that's been rusting away for thirty years. We run into that, we'll just find some tool and bust the welds; it's not kryptonite, you know."

The tunnel's grade began to slope down until the miniature rails submerged under a still, black pool of water. I stepped carefully into the pool feeling along one track with my toes. The further I went the higher the water became; finally, it began to flood over the tops of my dingos, filling the tall leather boots with icy water. Displaying an admirable level of stoicism, Larry slogged along behind me. Ron gingerly stepped off into the pool and began to almost howl indignantly. "Jeez, Dewy, it's ice-cold!"

By then the rails had begun to surface. I shined the light back across the pool and saw Ron standing ankle-deep, looking up at another iron circle. A glance at my wristwatch: already 1:10 a.m. We had time, but we didn't have all night. "I never said it was going to be easy. You're going to be standing there all by your lonesome if you don't get the lead out."

Grumbling, Ron waded across the murky pool, stumbling halfway across, barely catching himself before he fell face-first into the water. "God, Dewy, I can't believe you talked me into this. How much farther is it?"

"A good ways."

The rail bed angled back up, and now we began to pass small side chambers. Some had small bricked-up entrances in the back, and a few had steel double doors welded shut.

"Looks like we're getting into town. That's where they used to dump coal directly into the basements to feed the furnaces. We're getting closer to the end."

We blundered along in the dark for another twenty minutes when the tunnel abruptly widened out, finally stopped by a wall of red brick bound with crumbling mortar. A stout iron ladder ran up the brick, stopping a foot short of another round iron plate. We played the lights along the circular edge; you could see the sharp cracks of broken metal, and someone had broken the rim free of the casing. I sat my old pack on the ground and dug around in it until I found a paper containing a lump of burnt cork. I began to smear the carbonized cork on my nose and chin. The boys looked at me like I was suddenly putting on a minstrel show. "It's to cut the reflection of light off your face. Want some?"

Ron shook his head, Larry nodded, and then they were both smearing each other's faces. After they finished I put the cork away, slung the pack onto my back and stepped up on the ladder. Bracing myself, I placed both hands in the middle of the iron cover and shoved with all my strength. It budged just enough to allow a ray of yellowish streetlight to peep under. I caught the whiff of garbage and shoved it again. This time I was able to inch the heavy cover to the side. Another effort and it became a little easier. Finally, I was able to grasp it by the edge and slide it away onto the pavement.

I eased my head through the hole until my eyes were at street level. It was just like Red Tuttle had claimed; we were in an alley behind one of the businesses that ring the central courthouse square. Downtown was as still as a tombstone. I glanced at my watch: 2:00 a.m. This was as dead as it was ever going to get. I was up and out, then pressing myself against a brick wall. Larry and Ron flopped out of the hole and followed suit. After another look up and down the alley, we huddled. Even though the air was dry and cool, our faces shone with sweat through the burnt cork.

I issued orders quickly. "Ron, you go down to the end of the alley and hunker down behind those garbage cans. Larry, go back up to the other end where you can see the city garage. If either of you boys sees Chief Morgan out snooping around, give me a long blink on the light, and I'll go to ground. Give two short blinks when he's gone. I'm going to loop around and make sure no one is working late. Got it?"

Then I was off, slinking down a narrow side alley, dashing from cover to cover until I could see a corner of the courthouse building. I eased down the wall and cautiously peeped around the corner, almost hoping the robot was gone.

The Gort was still there, standing motionless in the same spot it had silently occupied for three decades. I could just see the cluster of garbage cans where I hoped Ron was still on station. I gave a long single flash and waited for what seemed like an hour. I was beginning to think he had run out on me, but then a small yellow dot of light blossomed and faded. I relaxed; Ron had checked with Larry first, and it had taken a few seconds for the reply. Since the first time I had dreamed the stunt up, I was feeling a little tingle of fear, then suddenly I felt a little embarrassed for it. The Gort was nothing but a gigantic scarecrow for humans, and I was going to prove that for a fact, once and for all.

I took one more look around the square and ran for the cover of a boxwood hedge that bordered the long flight of steps leading to the front entrance of the courthouse. Crawling under the boxwoods, I held my light up and gave another flash. The answer came back almost immediately. Good for Ron and Larry; they were still committed to the mission. The next dash took me under the shadow of the Bulldog, an ancient six-pounder bronze cannon mounted on a crude angle-iron frame set into donated concrete. Captured by the Tallulah County rifles in Mexico, it had been brought back as a trophy and had seen action twenty years later at Mud Creek with Bedford Forrest. Hidden after the surrender, it had been rediscovered, buried under an old barn, and unveiled as a memorial in 1905.

The Gort was only a hundred feet away now. I gave Ron a long single flash and waited for a reply. Nothing. I didn't think he had run out on me, not at this point, not when he had to face me in homeroom on Monday morning. I began to worry about his batteries. Lying under the Bulldog until dawn wasn't a viable option, and I had just broken cover when the warning came: two short flashes, a pause, then two more for emphasis. Then I saw the reflection of headlights off the big picture windows of Corner Hardware and threw myself flat on the short grass of the lawn. Morgan's hulking patrol car slowly turned the corner and began to roll down Main Street at a blazing ten miles an hour.

My heart thumped like a kettledrum in my chest as Morgan's car drifted closer. He was so near, I could hear the faint strains of a Hank Williams song and smell the cigarette butt he flipped out the window, exploding on the curb in a burst of red sparks only twenty feet away. I held my breath waiting for him to shine the spotlight on my face, wondering what I was going to say when he grabbed me up by the nape of the neck and asked me what in the Sam Hill I was doing here at 2:00 a.m. Then he was past my position and making a lazy loop around the town square. He stopped at the nearest corner, and I tried to wish myself invisible, processed with the notion I had been spotted, or at least he could hear my heart thumping on the ground. The crackle of a two-way radio drowned out Williams, and I saw Morgan talking into a boxy microphone.

The red bubble on top of the patrol car began to flash, and Morgan roared away the way he had come. The pulsing red light and wailing siren faded away; there was a long single flash from the lookout. It was now or never. I sprinted toward the white picket fence like my britches were on fire, vaulting over the points and rolling as I landed on a soft bed of new mulch, grunting with pain as the junk in my pack dug into my back. I slipped the rucksack off and undid the buckles, heartened by the fouled anchor and globe of the United States Marine Corps, fading away but still visible on the top flap. Pulling out the paint can, I rolled over and gazed up at the robot. I had forgotten how big it was.

One thing was for sure, I had a target too big to miss, and the machine's ass was as broad as the back hatch of the barf barge. Shaking the can to mix the paint, I stopped and held my breath, looking back the way Morgan had gone. The plastic ball rattling around in the can echoed off the storefronts like a machine gun in church. A quick glance at my lookout. Nothing. I gave another shake and stood before the robot's hind end. I couldn't get over how big it was. I had grown up seeing it on the courthouse square, but for the first time, I really had an appreciation of its massive body. Its butt was at face level, at least six feet off the ground. Its broad torso, sewer pipe arms, and bucket-like head cast enough shadow to hide a Cape buffalo. Holding the can upside down, I gave a little squirt to clear the nozzle and went to work.

I didn't rush the job. Spraying the letters in broad even strokes, I was pleasantly surprised to see that Mom had been right. This shit would stick to anything. It went onto the robot's ass like it was made from illustration board. No runs, no drips, and I even got the spelling right. G…O…R…T'S B…U...T...T! It only took a few seconds, and when I was done, I stepped back a few feet to admire my work. Even at night, I could see the glitter sparkle through the painted words. I liked it so much, I laughed so loud I startled myself a little. But no one was listening or watching but my own crew. **GORT'S BUTT!**

That was pretty good, but I felt like it needed something else — enough to get proper credit but not enough to get busted. Then I had a sudden inspiration. By now I had gotten a little bolder. I gave the can of Testbed metal-flake purple another shake and wrote another line in smaller letters just below the first. **Go Bulldogs!**

After another glance around the town square, I still had the all-clear. I was both exhilarated and more than a little amazed. The message stood out on the machine's butt like a purple neon sign. If Gort had been standing in the middle of the sticks, his ass would have lit up the countryside like a backwoods honky-tonk. I tossed the can back into the pack and gave a long single flash at Ron's position. I was answered by two long flashes that sent me down behind the Gort's angular feet. Then another long single flash, followed by a short blink. What the hell was that? Did they spot a threat that disappeared? What was the short flash?

I waited a few moments until I finally decided Ron had gotten a little confused. He was a hell of a good guy but tended to be a little dim sometimes. Pack in hand, I darted from behind the robot and ran for the alley like I was being chased by the demons of hell. I heard muffled clunking behind me and was halfway to cover before I was able to turn to see a short round object lying on the ground, smack between the robot and the street. The spray paint can wasn't just a can of spray paint; it was evidence. Any misgivings I had about going back after the can were blown away by the fear of discovery and its repercussions. I sprinted back to the can intending to scoop it up in one fluid motion, but instead it popped away like a loose football, clattering on the sidewalk with enough racket to wake the city cemetery.

I forced myself to take a long, deep breath and deliberately bent to grab it when the warning came. It wasn't two flashes of silent yellow light; it was Ronnie's terrified voice. "Dewy! Look out! It's waking up! Run, Dewy! Run!"

I glanced up, and what I saw robbed me of my wits. Even though my brain was screaming for me to flee for my life, my feet refused to listen. Looking back on that moment, my paralysis was understandable; after all, there are not many folks who have seen what I was looking at and lived to tell about it. The Gort's visor was open. There was that tiny hot point of light racing back and forth on the Gort's head like a bee caught in a pickle jar. I knew what it meant. Everyone on planet Earth knew what the dancing light meant: that rascal was getting ready to shoot. There was no point in running or dodging or diving behind a fire hydrant for cover. I could be standing ten miles away and the machine could nail me with no more effort than me shooting a gallon milk jug sitting on a stump. For an ephemeral instant, the bouncing white light stopped and we locked eye to eyes. It was at that moment that I discovered something no other Earthling has ever known: I knew the Gort for what it was. I knew from where the Gort drew its infinite power. The Gort fired.

Like the atomic bomb, the power of the robot is impossible to comprehend from grainy old newsreels. Unless you've seen it firsthand, a person can't fathom the concentrated power of the Gort. A blinding, arrow-straight line about the width of a strand of spider silk instantly connected the paint can to the machine's head. The can flared up into a translucent glow, then faded into a pale smear of elemental dust on the lawn. I fell backward and landed hard on my butt. Lurching to my feet, I bolted for the alley as the vivid image of a long-ago sermon swirled up from the abyss of memory.

It was about Lot's incredibly impulsive wife — so dimwitted they didn't even bother to record her name. She had been favored and blessed by God. She and her family had been delivered from a wicked people and their doomed city with the help of two angels sent by Jehovah. Given ample help by the Lord, they made good their escape into the surrounding desert wilderness in the shallowest nick of time. They had gotten free and clear as the twin cities of Sodom and Gomorrah were incinerated behind them. She must have known instinctively what was happening. She would have been able to feel the heat burning through her robes like the flash of a nuclear weapon, but she was safe. All the damn fool woman had to do was follow the very clear instructions: do not look back. So like a complete idiot, she stopped, turned to look, and was promptly transformed into a pillar of rock salt. She and I must have been cut from the same halfwit cloth.

I stopped and turned back to look. The Gort's visor was still open but the beam of energy had retracted back to a single dancing point of light. The point grew bigger and I was suddenly encircled with an uncomfortable hot light that blotted out all other senses, except a painful scorching of my right hand and fingers. For a split second, I wondered if this was what it was like to be dead. Then I could see and hear again, but I felt like I had fallen off the roof of my house. I looked down and saw a pile of glowing dust at my feet. The robot had destroyed the pack in my hand. The light began to dance again and that got me moving. We'll never know if Lot's wife, given the chance, would have been dumb enough to steal a second look, but I sure as heck wasn't. Diving for the open hole in the pavement, I felt frantically for the iron rungs and went zooming down, landing hard on the tracks of the subterranean railroad, saved from a broken back only by the rubbery bones of youth.

I took off running down the tunnel until I began to collide with the walls. I had to stop and catch my wind before the terrible truth of the situation hit me. My flashlight had been in the old rucksack. Now it was just a drifting pile of grey dust, and I was alone in the dark. I heard a faint echo above my wheezing lungs and caught the barest gleams of light far ahead in the tunnel. Then they were gone. The boys were way ahead of me. I gave a wordless indignant yell that bounced down the black tunnel like a damned soul.

I cussed them every inch of that wet, dirty wall as I felt my way along it for the best part of two miles. I splashed, stumbled, and boiled with anger the entire distance, looking back every few feet, half expecting the Gort to have somehow squeezed its massive body into the tunnel with me, but there was no sign of pursuit. The further I went, the less fear I had of the robot and more fury at my alleged pals. My path was lit by the lamp of anger, my feet guided by thoughts of justified vengeance, and my blood simmered with the sweet heat of impending payback. I'd hog-tie every one of them, paint their nuts blue, and dump them in the Tallulah wilderness for the bears and wild hogs to fight over. I'd put bags over their heads and deposit them in front of the Gort as a sacrifice in way of apology. Or I might just beat the snot out of them after school on Monday afternoon. But there would be a reckoning just as sure as God made little green apples.

Finally, I could see the barest trace of a lesser blackness ahead. My foot kicked something that clanked and clattered, and I knew I was home free; I had stumbled into the skeleton of that nameless unfortunate horse. Groping my way past the rotting coal train, I emerged into the open where, not surprisingly, nobody was waiting. Stomping through the abandoned coal yard, I felt a cool drop of water splash on my face, followed by another and another. By the time I made it to the dilapidated office building, the water was hammering down like a cow pissing on a flat rock. Then an engine gunned to life and I was in a bubble of yellowish light. For a split second I thought the Gort was lying in ambush for me, but the barge rolled from cover and lurched to a stop in front of me.

Bob pulled the cracked driver's side window down with one hand and leaned out as casually as if we had been in the church parking lot after choir practice. "Hey, Dewy, you need a ride back to camp?" After a good look at my face, he seemed a little less cheerful. "Boy, you looked like you been shot at and missed but shit at and hit."

I struggled with the passenger door until he leaned across to give it a good thump with an open palm. The barge opened up for me, and I collapsed onto the lumpy bench seat. As the barge turned onto the paved road, I could hear stray parts rattle around in the doors.

Bob gave me a cagey look. In those days, I had quite the reputation for a hot temper. We were back on hard pavement heading back to Spanish Fields before he said anything. "Say, Dewy, you look a fright. You want me to take you home?"

I growled like an irritated lion. "Where are they, Bob? That's where I want you to take me. I want you to take me to them."

The barge's one working windshield wiper fought a losing battle with the pounding rain, then stopped halfway across the windshield. Bob punched the switch and the wiper began to work again. "I don't know where they are, bud. They came running past me and just kept on going. I figured it was best to wait for you. Just about ready to get some help when you came along. You sure you're all right, Dewy? You look a fright. You want a beer?"

"You think I look bad now, wait till I get through with Ron and Larry."

Bob, an occasionally devoted Christian, shook his head in disapproval. "Now I don't think that will accomplish anything, Dewy. Let's go back to camp and get you cleaned up. We'll wait for a decent hour and head on back to town. You can wash off in the creek. I don't think you want to go home looking like that. We'll stop at Piggy's Truck Stop and get some breakfast. My treat. What do you say?"

I pulled down the passenger side sun visor. By some minor miracle the barge still had a working dime-sized light bulb above the mirror inside the visor. My face was encrusted with a nasty mix of coal dust and burnt cork, and there was a thin rim of dried blood along both nostrils that matched the color of my eyes. I held my right hand up to the light expecting to see the bones through charred meat, but there wasn't even a blister, just a black patina of coal dust ground into the skin and under the fingernails. Looking down, I could see that my lucky jacket had been stripped of every button, and the left sleeve was missing. I began to slide into the depths of an almost irretrievable melancholy. I had ruined my lucky jacket. "You think a couple of scrambled eggs and a slice of country ham will make up for this?"

He shrugged. "It won't hurt. I know that belonged to your pa, but it's just an old jacket. Main thing is … say, I almost forgot … did you do it?"

"Do what?"

"Tag the Gort? Did the paint stick?"

"Like a wad of chewing gum on the bottom of your shoe."

I looked into the little mirror and smiled; my teeth were as bright against my skin as the light from Gort's head. Suddenly things didn't seem so bad. In exchange for getting dirty, ruining my jacket, and losing my pack, I had gained a morsel of knowledge no one else in the world had. The Permanent Peace might keep us boxed up down here on Earth, but they have been forthcoming with information about the universe — folks that swim in chlorine atmospheres and planets that orbit around marble stars. Now I knew what gave the Gort such God-like powers and why the Permanent Peace deferred to any and all decisions the robots made. It's hard to disagree with something that holds a dwarf star captive in its head.

There was no homeroom for anyone on Monday morning. Any person who hadn't smelled trouble from the pack of strange cars that had taken over teacher parking got an education the second they entered the building. Everyone was directed to the assembly hall by scowling teachers.

To take their customary seats, it was seniors up front, juniors just behind them, and so on back to the two rows in the rear filled with pimply ninth-graders. I sat in the middle of the front row where I had a ringside view of our principal's pallid face. I had never liked Principal Williams, and the feeling was mutual, but now I couldn't help but spare a little pity for the man, and almost a little guilt for putting him up there.

He began without introductions or preambles while a line of Alabama state troopers and black-suited government types sat behind him. Normally, my heart would have skipped a few beats when Williams spared an analytical stare at me, but now he didn't seem nearly as intimidating as he had before my close encounter with an alien robot. Then he passed over me to spread the dirty looks across the crowd. The homeroom bell rang on schedule and the 'hearing' was called to order.

He always held forth with enough volume for the Senate floor. We called him Colonel Foghorn. "I won't beat around the bush. Saturday night or early Sunday morning someone defaced the Gort stationed in our little town — with a can of spray paint. This is a very serious matter."

After a thundering understatement like that, the student body was all silent attentiveness — no whispers, giggles, or palmed notes, just a cavernous howl of silence. He let the words hang over us like an anvil dangling by a cotton string. Everyone leaned forward in their seats to catch the next dramatic revelation. I endeavored to look as innocently stupid as the ninth-graders. Beady-eyed troopers and federal agents scanned the crowd for clues to the identity of the reckless vandals. Occasionally, one would be on me for a couple of terrifying seconds before moving on to someone else.

"We have every reason to believe that it was a member of the student body who did this awful thing. As you can see, this senseless criminal act is being investigated by both state and federal authorities."

Poor Chief Morgan. He had been cut from the roster of investigators with little or no fanfare. Maybe they considered him a suspect. That actually did make me feel guilty; he and my dad had been fishing buddies, and Morgan had always been kind to me.

After letting the information on investigations sink in, Colonel Foghorn continued. "The authorities have been quite reasonable about this. If this vandalism was indeed committed by one or more of our students, as we have reason to believe, we're going to give you a chance to turn yourselves in. If you do so, things will go a lot easier for all concerned. If anyone here knows the identity of these vandals, it is your moral duty to turn them in."

I felt like I was standing in a one-man police lineup for the murder of Abe Lincoln. I snatched glances at Ron, Larry and Bob; both were staring at the principal with pale but stoically unreadable faces. I already knew they were just bullshitting us. If they had a positive ID, they wouldn't have waited until Monday to grab a suspect.

Williams continued with his booming riverboat gambler voice, about to slap his royal flush onto the table and rake it all in. "I want all of you to know that a can of paint matching the color used to deface the Gort was found on the courthouse lawn. It's being analyzed for fingerprints in a government laboratory this very minute."

I couldn't help myself; it was a form of ballistic laughing diarrhea. I had no more control over that lone snort of disbelief than I would have over amoebic dysentery. Taking fingerprints? From what? Fingerprints my ass. I took a deep breath and tried hard to look serious, but I couldn't ditch the knowing smirk. Foghorn glared at me while a line of red crept up his neck and crawled over his face like a cartoon thermometer. He pointed a stubby white finger at me; those of us who were close enough could see his hand shaking. Everyone within earshot could hear the fear in his voice. It couldn't have happened to a more deserving man. "I don't think you youngsters understand that these men represent the Permanent Peace and —"

He never finished the sentence. For once in his career, Colonel Foghorn was drowned out by something even louder than he was: an auditorium full of grades nine through twelve. It was a spontaneous outburst of derisive outrage that visibly angered the troopers and government types. All of us had grown up seeing reps from the Permanent Peace on TV, and some had even seen one in person on a field trip to Washington, DC. The real article has a dignified but friendly bearing, always polite. A rep from the Peace never threatens, but his words ring like an iron hammer in a silk glove. These boys were representatives of the Permanent Peace like a timber wolf is a sheepdog. We hooted and hollered so loudly that dust began to float down from the lighting fixtures! The cops looked as angry as Foghorn looked mortified.

Colonel Foghorn tried to restore order, and he did manage to quiet things back down, but the spell was broken. Any chance he had of ferreting out the delinquent artist evaporated when he made the ridiculous assertion that the goon squad seated behind him actually spoke for the spacemen. The president might be able to get away with doing it, but not a handful of strange cops, and certainly not a high school principal.

One of the government types, a flinty-faced man, got out of his chair and nearly pushed Williams aside as he took a position behind the podium. "I am Special Agent Clark from the United States Department of Justice. I don't think any of you young people understand the gravity of this situation! Each and every one of you is going to be individually interrogated until — " SCREEEEEEEEEEEEEE!

The public address system erupted in a howl of anguished feedback. The PA system had always been a little twitchy, but now it sounded like someone was pulling out its electronic fingernails. Agent Clark grabbed the goose-necked microphone to adjust its position, then yanked his hand back like he had been struck by a rattlesnake. Being right in the front row, I could see the hot blue spark that had jumped from the mic to his fingertips. It looked like a painful experience. Whatever his other faults as a human being, the man was determined to take control of the situation.

He leaned forward to the buzzing microphone and began again. "As I was saying — " SCREEEEEEEEEECH!

This time the spark lashed him across the face like a bright blue hickory switch and sent him reeling back to be caught by a pair of startled state troopers with excellent reflexes. The overhead lights went off as fire alarms throughout the building began to wail. I caught the scent of burning electronics just as the emergency lights flared to life. Above our heads, thin wisps of blue smoke were wandering around the dead lights.

Clark's junior partner seemed struck by indecision: help his pal or attempt to take control of the proceedings. I heard a commotion in the back of the auditorium. A single file of high school freshmen was being herded through the double doors into bright autumn light. The other homeroom teachers were sharp enough to take their cue and began, in their turn, to move their classes outside in an orderly manner.

I was one of the last seniors who filed out. Behind me, the troopers, feds, and Colonel Foghorn were having a spirited but pointless argument. Just as our homeroom teacher left the auditorium, the emergency lighting cut out and the fire alarm fell silent. The arguments behind us continued in a darkened auditorium.

Outside, it took a few moments for what had just happened to sink in. The traffic light at the intersection had died, but there wasn't any danger because every car and truck on the street sat motionless. A few drivers had already raised the hoods of their vehicles and were bent over the lifeless motors.

Larry pointed at the dead neon signs. "The power's off downtown, too." He shielded his eyes and looked into the sky. "I don't hear any thunder. A drunk might have plowed into the substation."

I shook my head. "What about cars and trucks? Wilson Dam could have collapsed but it wouldn't have knocked out all the traffic."

Larry shrugged. "Might be bad gas."

The 'inquisition' began to spill out, red-faced and bristling at everyone and everything around them.

Ron made another keen observation. "Oh my, Dewy, I bet you a coke it's happened again."

I played stupid. I didn't want to face the possibility that I might be responsible for the unfolding chaos. A bright yellow biplane buzzed over us, headed in the direction of the county airport. I pointed at the crop duster. "Close but no cigar. That boy's flying along just fine."

Ronnie was undeterred. "Just goes to prove my point. They say the first time it happened, hospital elevators got stuck between floors while the lights stayed on in the operating rooms. Ships in calm seas lost all power while ships in storms kept the propellers turning over. Airplanes on the runways wouldn't start, but planes in the air landed."

"Yeah, yeah, we all learned that in the third grade, but it doesn't mean it's happened again."

I must have sounded pretty annoyed because Bob and a few other kids began to gather around us. Bob made sure all the teachers were out of earshot before speaking. "Damnation, Dewy! It's happened again! I wonder if it's just here or all over the world."

"Would you two shut the heck up? The only thing that's happened is a surge on the power grid! They'll have the lights back on in an hour!"

Ron looked at the cars and trucks. Every one of them static as a park bench. "What about them cars?"

"Damnit, Ron! It's not them cars; it's those cars! No wonder you got a D in English."

I could feel my face getting red as a pickled beet while pearls of sweat burst out on my forehead. Ron stuck his hands in his pockets and stared at the ground as he kicked gravel with his toe. I felt like a grade Z heel.

"No reason for you to be mean to me. You can be so mean sometimes, Dewy."

I was about to apologize when an excited murmer went through the student body — class was dismissed for the day. We didn't wait around for them to have a change of heart. I felt a hand on my shoulder. It was Bob.

"Come on boys, let's ride down to the river and wet some hooks."

The anger had drained away. I felt tired, embarrassed, and a little worried. It wouldn't take a genius to make the connection between my behavior and the events of the day. "I guess you're right. I'm sorry I snapped at you, Ronnie." I looked around; nothing seemed any more mobile than it was when we came out of the building. "Looks like if we're gonna go fishing, we'll have to get out our bikes or hoof it."

In the school parking lot, a number of students were trying to start their cars but weren't having any more luck than anyone else.

Bob was undeterred. "If anything starts, it'll be the barge. We won't know till we try."

I shuffled along behind the boys to the parking lot where other students stood around their immobile vehicles, wondering what to do. For once the drivers watched the younger kids peddle away with a tinge of envy. Even the slickest hot rod was nothing now but a gigantic paperweight. Dashboard gauges indicated plenty of juice in everyone's batteries, but all radios were silent. By now I was feeling pretty cynical. It was only a matter of time until I was apprehended.

"You're wasting your time, Bob. Come on, let's go already."

Bob got behind the wheel of the barge, gave the steering column a couple of punches to wake up the starter, and turned the key. The barf barge roared to life in a cloud of oily smoke. Everyone in earshot stared at the barge like it was a blue whale that parachuted out of the sky. The 'inquisition' had forgotten its argument. Now the troopers, agents, and Colonel Foghorn studied us with open mouths and wide, white eyes. It was time to get while the gettin' was good.

Larry ran around to the passenger side. "I call shotgun!"

The fish hit like Babe Ruth for the rest of the day. The following Friday night the New Garnett Bulldogs were whipped senseless by the Rockport Raiders. My magnificent plan to gain an unbeatable psychological edge had been a total bust. But the fishing was better than anyone alive could remember.

Contempt is the least problematic thing bred by familiarity. Familiarity can lure you into complete apathy or foolhardy courage. Familiarity can make a job too easy, inducing you to get sloppy, cut corners, and get your ass in a serious jam. Familiarity can not only endanger you but also the people around you. Accused of familiarity, I would have to plead guilty, but so would everyone in the country — every soul in the world for that matter. The Permanent Peace hadn't put the hammer down for thirty years. Given enough time, events that had once turned the world upside down were now boring old history lessons that no one cared about anymore.

We had all gotten so used to the Permanent Peace that their blessings were almost taken for granted. The Gorts had been inactive so long that there was the popular conception that the machines were nothing but mock-ups, harmless as a toothless old poodle.

Any familiarity I had felt toward the Permanent Peace had vanished with Planter's visit. The familiarity the townsfolk had felt toward me after his visit went up like spit on a hot stove.

At first, I rather liked it. Not a single person had the nerve to ask what the visit had been about and that's just the way I intended to keep it. Before Planter came to visit, I had nearly reached the conclusion that I had been in the job a little too long. Even when I arrested someone for a serious crime, I had the feeling they were just going along with me because, well, because I was me. With fewer than five thousand citizens, New Garnett still had more people than I could know, but they all knew me. They knew I wasn't above giving someone a second chance, or even a third or fourth chance. I did this for practical reasons. Like the old saying goes, you demand an eye for an eye and a tooth for a tooth, and pretty soon we're all blind and need dentures. Now folks treated me with a differential respect bordering on fear.

They finally came on Friday morning. I had promised myself I would end my fishing trip by 7 a.m. and be at work at 8 a.m. sharp, but the weather was nice, fish were biting, and it was a quarter til before I could pull myself away from the weed beds. I stopped at Alex's Bait Shop on the way back in to show off the day's catch and ice down a mix of pan-sized bluegills and sunfish. If everyone in town could behave for a few hours, I'd take a long lunch, clean the fish, and store them in the freezer. When I pulled into my parking slot, I saw that unruly locals would be the least of my worries that day. Tribulation had arrived in two of the hulking sport trucks the federals prefer. All black glass and four-wheel drive, they had parked smack dab on the yellow curb, fire hydrant and Gort be damned.

The instant I walked into the courthouse, Shelia dashed out of the revenue department and grabbed me by the arm. After ten years of working county and city tax collection, there's not a lot you can say or do to intimidate the woman, but now her voice sounded like I was suffering a fatal heart attack.

"There's five of them, Dewy. I tried to make them wait for you, but they just ignored me and broke into your office. Jim and Carol are on a call out in the county and the dispatcher says the radio isn't working. There was no one here to stop them."

I gave her a reassuring little pat on the arm. "Nothing they could have done anyway but get into a mess with the feds. Don't worry Shelia, I'll handle them all right. They probably just want to ask for directions to a good fishing hole."

She went back into her office and I trotted up the stairs. I could hear them taking the place apart from the first floor. The crash of glass echoed down the hall, and I instinctively brushed my fingertips along the bulk of a holstered Slimline .45. Although it's consistently denied at the highest levels, a few words with a Neighbor can indeed result in a long detention with no charges. I wasn't so much surprised by the visit as by the fact it had taken so long for them to get around to it. But, New Garnett is fifty miles from the nearest interstate, and as far as I knew, the federals didn't know we had rebuilt after the war. One thing is for sure, over the past century they had lost none of their talent for destruction. I watched them pillage my desk and closet for thirty seconds before they spotted me. Arrogant, unprofessional familiarity. I could have nailed all five of them with three rounds to spare if I had been so inclined. I knocked loudly on the door, now dangling forlornly from its bottom hinge.

"Hello, boys. Ya'll lookin' for something?"

Their boss was built like a fireplug with a face that was all slabs, wrinkles, and little snaky eyes. He was sitting in my chair like he had bought it at a yard sale. His men looked up and pulled out identical weapons with smooth, practiced moves. A tall, skinny agent flashed chromed steel rings, but his boss held up one finger. He knew he had the advantage over me; there was no hurry. There was plenty of time to cuff me and toss a black bag over my head. Then they could question me at leisure back in Atlanta. He got right down to business.

"I'm Special Agent Vanzetti with Federal Internal Security. We have information you were contacted by, and spent time with, a representative of the Permanent Peace. Is that true?"

I kept my hands in plain view. "Sure, no law against talking to one is there?"

Vanzetti was unimpressed. "There might be. Depends on what you were discussing. What did you talk about?"

I shrugged. "Small talk, fishing, hunting, how the Crimson Tide was shaping up for next season. You know, man stuff. Or maybe you don't. He went to a crime scene with me to make observations and see some real police work. You should try it yourself sometime."

Well, no cop likes a smart mouth and he sure didn't like mine. He stood up and placed both palms on the desk while two agents got behind me. The other two just kept digging through my stuff like blind hogs rooting for acorns.

"I find it difficult to believe a Neighbor went this far off the main roads to talk to some hick sheriff about football."

"I'm not a hick sheriff; I'm a hick detective. And I may be a hick, but I know enough about my profession to get a warrant before I go digging through someone else's property. I also know how to knock."

"We don't need a damn piece of paper to protect the country, and you know it. Are you armed?"

"Sure, part of the job. Run into tough guys like you all the time."

"Place your weapon on the desk, please. Slowly."

I gingerly laid the Slimline in front of him. He shook his head and rolled his eyes. "You're rather old-fashioned. I suppose that's the kind of thing we can expect down here."

"Don't care for a plasma pistol. It's like shooting a damn flamethrower that runs out of gas too quick. That's one reason they don't give us more technology, you know. Some jerk always wants to use it to burn off someone else's head."

"That's not your concern. Agent Smalls, empty his pockets."

Smalls patted me down with a quick, practiced hand and tossed my own cuffs, spare magazine, and wallet onto my desk. He dug around in my front left pocket and relieved me of a switchblade I had confiscated on my first night as a rookie and carried ever since. Tossing the knife onto the desk, he plunged into my right pocket and immediately found himself face up on the floor. His mouth worked wordlessly until he managed a thin gasp of pained disbelief, staring at the white smoke curled up from his blackened fingertips. It must have hurt like the fires of hell, because it sucked the wind right out of his sails.

I pulled out the card before anyone got their wits back. It glowed as hot as the burning bush of Moses, and like the bush, my hand was not consumed. The cherry-red card was now graced with the stylized outline of a Gort etched with the absolute blackness of deep space. I was as shocked as the man sitting on the floor sucking on his scorched fingers, but I have enough sense to know when the opportunity of salvation presents itself. I dangled the red hot card in front of Vanzetti and his slack-jawed crew like a lucky rabbit's foot.

"Do you know what this is, tough guy?"

Before he could answer, there was a woman's piercing scream from outside and the screech of burning rubber. We all looked out the tall window and saw that, for the first time since its arrival, Gort had moved; now it was standing in the middle of the street next to an abandoned Volkswagen that had jumped the curb. A few clumps of citizens were pointing and jabbering at the robot, but most folks had already gone to cover. For a long speechless moment, we all stared at the robot. The visor was already open and you could see that blinding speck of celestial light running back and forth inside its head. The brilliant speck stopped and then leaped out to bathe one of the FIS trucks in a searing beam of pure light. The beam's energy spread over the truck's body in a thin glowing skin. Despite brilliant midday sunshine, black shadows ran across the whole town. When we uncovered our eyes, the vehicle was only a layer of pale grit on the pavement.

I casually walked over to the desk and began to retrieve my

goods, holstering my pistol and retrieving my wallet. The ones still on their feet stared at the robot as it struck the other vehicle, reducing it to pale talcum — fine drifts of atomic dust.

"Well boys, looks like you've got a long walk ahead of you. Tell you what, I'll see if Sam will ride you out to the county line in the animal control wagon, then you're on your own from there. Normally I tell visitors to come back anytime, but in your case that might be unwise. Now git."

His men shot out my busted door like scalded monkeys, but to his credit, the boss was made of sterner stuff. Vanzetti stood his ground, for a few moments anyway.

"You'll live to regret that, you damn redneck!"

I smiled, all wide-eyed innocence. Now it was fun. "Regret what, Special Agent Vanzetti?"

"Siccing your robot on us! You damn people haven't changed a bit! You're still nothing but a gang of ignorant inbred traitors —"

I've developed a thick skin over the years, but that made me furious. I nabbed Vanzetti by the nape of the neck and hauled him back to the window. We both watched the Gort clomp back inside its little white picket fence, close its visor, and turn around to face the street. Somehow the camellias had been brushed aside and the legend on the robot's backside was there for the entire world to read.

Vanzetti pointed with a quivering finger at the metal-flake purple words. "Someone's defaced the robot."

"Listen to me, you little pissant! Nobody controls the Gorts but the Gorts! They're here for a reason, and that's to protect the world from nasty little shits like you! Now get the hell out of my town before I toss your sorry ass into a padded cell and call my friends."

I relieved him of the plasma pistol while I talked, then grabbed him by the belt and bum-rushed him to the top of the stairs. Vanzetti must have thought I was going to toss him down to the next landing because he broke free and bounced away like a loose basketball. Back at the window, I watched him jump into the deserted VW, back off the curb, and tear down the street for a hundred feet before it died. I had almost decided to pick him up for car theft when he bailed out of the bug and took off at a speed that was remarkable for a man with such short legs.

I was still sweeping up broken glass when Mr. Planter pecked gently on my broken office door.

"Hello, Detective Law, is everything all right?"

Still wearing the same neutral suit and impassive face, he could have passed for someone selling brushes door to door. I held one finger to my lips and prayed that the universal sign for silence was truly universal. "Yeah, everything's fine. I think the guys that did this were in the wrong place."

I scribbled quickly on a yellow legal pad with a black marker; surely he could at least read English. I held the pad up with both hands; the message was simple and direct. 'Careful. We may be bugged!'

Reading my frantic note, he questioned me with those unnervingly hazel eyes. I frantically posted a more specific note.'We are under surveillance. Watch what you say!'

"Just call me Dewy. What can I do for you today?"

Planter smiled broadly, pulled a squat silver cylinder from his pocket, and popped off a cap of soft, translucent material. He upended the cylinder and dumped onto my desk a pile of short, black wires, along with a few grimy, dark plastic discs perforated with small holes. "I'm quite confident it's safe for you and me to speak plainly. I took the liberty of sweeping this building recently for hidden listening devices. I found quite an assortment."

He held up a thin springy wire the length of a shotgun shell with a bulbous end the size of a kitchen match. "I found a good many of these. They are derived from technology given to all of this world's governments but intended for medical use. I am disappointed that our gift has been misused, but I am no longer surprised by such things."

I picked up one of the larger objects. It was like the lower half of a miniature telephone receiver and had two copper leads dangling out of the back. The other was similar but even chunkier. "These aren't yours, are they?"

He smiled and shook his head. "I don't think so."

I turned the wastebasket right side up and tossed the ancient Bakelite bugs into the trash.

"Looks like President Garfield didn't quite trust us yet. They must have been recording our seditious conversations with wax cylinders. Think there's any more?"

"No, I had the Gort to verify that I found them all."

There was no point in asking when he/they had swept the building for bugs. He might have done the job last night, or he might have done the job between the ticks of a clock. With these jokers, you never knew.

"Well, at any rate, thanks for backing me up. Hadn't been for you and the Gort, I'd be on my way to Atlanta right now, hog-tied and with a sack on my head."

He shook his head in a matter-of-fact way. "The Gort was watching the whole time in the event you needed assistance. A good thing it was."

"I suppose the robot never sleeps."

"The Gort can remain motionless for centuries but is always constantly on the alert. Today is the first time one on Earth has been activated in several decades. Dewy, I'm very happy you and everyone else here escaped unscathed, but that's not really the primary reason why I'm here. There is something going on that has us all deeply concerned. Its about the uh … reconstructions?"

"The reconstructions?"

"I think that's the term. Large groups of people, almost all male, reconstructing and simulating historical military conflicts."

"Ohhhh, you mean the reenactors?"

"Yes, yes, that's it, the reenactors. What they may well do is provoke one of the Gorts to take action if it thinks open warfare has broken out. You know we have no control over the robots. They cooperate with us, but we do not issue instructions. Are you aware reenactors have become a worldwide movement? Groups in Europe, Asia, and the Americas are recreating wars of the past. By now these conflicts should be forgotten altogether."

"Sure I am. They've got their own hit TV show, and *Blast from the Past* is the most popular show in the country right now, plus about a thousand spin-offs. Mr. Planter, I don't think you should pay too much attention to them. It's just an escapist costume fantasy. It's like some kids in the attic dressing up with old clothes and pretending to be grown-ups. There's no real danger of conflict here.

As far as warfare being forgotten, it won't be forgotten until out of living memory, after my generation has died off."

"But you are far too young to have fought in the last human conflicts."

I pointed at the picture of my father, the young, old man with shadowed eyes hiding terrible secrets only he and his comrades had known. "I grew up in a house where we always left the hallway lights on at night. If he woke up in a darkened house, Daddy would fly into a near panic. Late one night, when I was about thirteen or fourteen, a thunderstorm woke me up. It had knocked out the electricity, and a darkened house was a real novelty to me. So I got up to explore and see what it was like. When I went into the kitchen, someone grabbed me from behind, threw me down, and put a butcher knife to my throat."

Planter was horrified. "Was it an intruder? A burglar?"

"No, it was my father. My mom showed up in the nick of time and busted a lamp over his head. She not only gave me my life, she saved my life. So you see, even though I was born years after the Japanese surrender, that conflict traveled ten thousand miles to my home in the middle of the night and damn near killed me. It was the only time I had ever seen him cry. He blubbered all night. He got worse after that."

"I'm sorry, Dewy, that's something we never thought of. Is he better now, your father?"

"Depends on what you believe. He died when I was sixteen; the official cause of death was death by misadventure — a hunting accident, they said. That way we got the life insurance and had enough money to live on. We knew better though. He suffered from wounds most folks couldn't see, and the pain from those wounds caused him to take his own life. I like to think he is now safe and happy in the care of the Lord, but like I said, it depends on what you believe. I once had a kid in the tenth grade tell me that everyone knew he had killed himself, and he went to hell because of it."

Planter seemed both sympathetic and fascinated. "It was needlessly cruel for him to do so. Out of curiosity, how did you react?"

"I pounced on him like a rabid wolf and started beating the

living shit out of him right there in the school lunchroom. He broke a water glass over my head, and that really pissed me off. It took the coach and two of our biggest football players to pull me off before I could kill him. That's when I got my reputation as a hot head, but one thing for sure, nobody ever messed with me after that."

"I imagine you must have been severely punished. Were you scourged?"

"Scourged? Look friend, this isn't imperial Rome. They just sent me home for a week and when I came back to school, they tried to recruit me for the football team. I told them thanks but no thanks."

He sighed like someone who had experienced a terrible disappointment, but he recovered his composure quickly. "I must return to the subject of the reenactors. I am given to understand there is to be a major reenactment here in your community this spring."

I nodded, happy to be off such an agonizing subject. "That's right, this April first; it's going to mark the one-hundred-and-tenth anniversary of the Battle of Garnett, one of the last stand-up fights of the American Civil War. To be honest, why anyone would want to commemorate it is way beyond me. Anyone with a lick of sense knew the war was nearly over and that we had gotten the dirty end of the stick, but they went ahead and fought it anyway."

Now he was Planter the historian. "What happened in the Battle of Garnett?"

"Nothing much to tell, really. We were pretty far off the main rail lines, so this was one of the last areas of the South to be invaded by Yankee troops. There was a one-legged brigadier general by the name of Roddy, who commanded a small garrison of local militia, and the boy must have taken his job right serious. When the Yankee commander demanded the surrender of the town along with all Confederate forces, Roddy replied with a shot from the Bulldog. Local lore claims that that shot cut the head clean off the Yankee commander's brother-in-law and severely wounded several others. When that happened, there was no going back and the fight was on."

"Bulldog?"

"Yeah, that's what we call the old cannon on the front lawn. The fight lasted most of the day, and when Roddy was finally shot off his crutches, resistance crumbled. After the surviving Rebels were scattered, the Yanks burned the old town right down to the foundations, just for spite. That's why we call it New Garnett. Old Garnett was razed to the ground. Somehow a few Rebs got the Bulldog away and buried it under an old barn. The gun was rediscovered in 1905, and it's been on the courthouse lawn ever since as a memorial. People just wanted to forget about the whole sorry business until the reenactors came along. When the chamber of commerce realized how much money it could bring in, they really started to get behind it. Now it's bigger than the watermelon festival."

"Dewy?"

"Yes?"

"May I have a cup of coffee?"

That made me feel a little better about things. I was starting to think Planter might be as human as the rest of us. "Sure thing, friend. Milk and sugar?"

He smiled like a schoolboy offered the entire bag of candy. "Both, please. One thing, Dewy."

"What's that?"

"If you ever meet any of my associates, I would appreciate it greatly if you did not mention that I have developed a fondness for the coffee drink."

"And especially coffee with a shot of milk, right?"

"Correct."

"Don't worry, pal, your secret's safe with Dewy Law. You watch my back and I watch yours."

If he suspected at that point that I knew the secret of the Gort's power, he didn't let on. Knowledge is a good thing unless it gets you kidnapped, tortured, and held in secret detention until the crack of doom.

We sipped coffee while he helped me clean up my wrecked office. When the last trash bag was full of broken glass, we topped off our cups and went outside to visit the Gort. Blind Bill nodded pleasantly at us as we walked past his stand, and I began to wonder how old he was. I made a mental note to check Bill's employment records. Only providence knew how far past retirement age he was.

"Dewy, how would you suggest we go about discouraging this activity?"

I shrugged. "The best thing to do is ignore it. Sooner or later people will get bored with it and move on to something like hula hoops or dancing the Charleston."

"Doing nothing strikes me as irresponsible, on our part anyway."

Damn, hadn't these people learned anything? "I can see how it might look like that on the surface, but there is a quirk in human nature that has vexed religions, governments, and law enforcement since the dawn of civilization. You tell the average person they are absolutely forbidden to do so and so, and the first thing they're going to do is go off somewhere and give it a try. You crack down and the problem just grows at an exponential rate. Let me give you an example: years ago the consumption and sale of beverage alcohol was banned in this country. The people who put this policy into action meant well for the most part; alcohol caused a lot of damage to lives and society. They figured without it, things would be better for everyone."

He nodded, drained his cup, and held it out for a refill. "Sounds like a reasonable course of action."

I reminded myself to be patient. Sometimes this was like teaching a blindfolded dog to play the pipe organ. "Sure it sounds all right on the surface, but the results were just the opposite of what was intended. You just couldn't snap your fingers and wish it away. Millions of people still wanted a drink and were willing to do damn near anything to get one. Vast criminal organizations sprang up overnight to supply demand, and a low-intensity war simmered for about twenty years before the powers that be gave up on prohibition."

"So now the use of beverage alcohol is … legal? But what about the health hazards of consumption and other problems?"

"What about them? It's still not a patch on the chaos brought on by banning alcohol. You can still find a few dry counties around, mostly in the Deep South or Midwest. Even Tallulah County voted to go wet two years ago."

He sipped his coffee and looked at the Gort; a morning dove sat on its head cooing like a happy baby. After it flew away, I could see the robot was due for a wash and wax.

"I see, so you think the best thing to do is nothing?"

"Definitely. Look, there's no danger of the Gort becoming activated unless someone gets hurt, right? Well, no one gets hurt at the reenactments unless it's sunstroke brought on by wearing an authentic wool uniform or falling off a horse. More people get hurt worse at a high school football game than in one of these sham battles. Mr. Planter, I can assure you that everything will be kept under control." I tried another angle. "Now if you insist that we put a stop to it, I'll do my best to accommodate you, but at most it'll just move to another location. We'll lose the business and I'll get the blame. Enough people get pissed about it, I could lose my job."

"We don't want any of that to happen. You say you can keep these activities restricted to certain parameters. How so?"

"Because I'm the head referee, that's how. The city and county governments require that we ride herd on these jokers for safety and insurance reasons. Hell, if we just let them go about it their own way, they would be shooting mini balls at each other in about five minutes."

"I am familiar with atomic weapons and plasma beams, but what is a mini ball?"

I plucked a conical slug of lead out of the shattered frame on my desk and tossed it to him. He caught it with a smooth, flawless motion and held it up between thumb and forefinger to examine.

"It doesn't look very dangerous."

I indulged in a rueful laugh. "Don't let the size fool you. Shot from a rifled musket, they go about a thousand feet per second. It'll shatter an arm or leg like glass on concrete, if it doesn't just kill you outright. Mr. Carpenter was … er … killed by a similar projectile. You see those little dents on the surface?"

Planter looked more closely. "Yes, they look like bite marks."

"That's exactly what they are. It's jokingly referred to as a medicine bullet. You held it between your teeth against the agony while they cut off a mangled limb with a dull saw or dug out a ball with dirty knives. Medicine was right primitive then. They didn't have much to kill pain then, but opium and whiskey. And the Rebs were usually flat out of that. A guy found that one with a metal detector over at Spanish Fields where there was a hospital. I want you to keep that as a reminder of how far we've come and what's at stake if we ever backslide."

He placed it carefully in his pocket. "Thank you, Dewy. I have some colleagues who may find this object quite enlightening."

I watched a grey pigeon light momentarily on the Gort's simplistic head. Before flapping away, it left behind a dirty white streak that slowly ran down the back. I gave Planter my best "bad cop" look. "You want to get enlightened, bring your pals down here come next April Fool's Day, and we'll give them something new to think about."

He nodded and handed me the empty cup. "Sounds reasonable. What is April Fool's Day?"

The first day of April dawned as soft as a baby's cheeks. The weather had only really started to break for the better a few weeks before, but the woods were already splashed with geysers of dogwood blooms and carpets of butter-yellow daffodils. The low hills overlooking Spanish Fields were speckled with picnickers who had the best spots staked out since before sunrise. By 9 a.m., it was standing room only. Even New Year's fireworks didn't draw crowds this big. I could even see kids up in the trees straining to get a better look at the show. The mayor and the local chamber of commerce were beside themselves with glee; the town's two hotels were packed, and hungry tourists stood in long lines outside every restaurant in town.

As a citizen of New Garnett, I should have been thrilled too, but I've always had a tough time working up any enthusiasm for these things. There were all the usual long-winded speeches about honoring our gallant ancestors and keeping history alive, but why anyone would go to so much trouble to celebrate the largest mass murder in American history is lost on me. I once read that after the Battle of Gettysburg, there were an estimated six million pounds of dead meat scattered on the battlefield. Three thousand tons of rotting humans, mules, and horses stank things up so bad that anyone who hadn't fled the area carried bottles of peppermint oil with them for relief. The town was uninhabitable until the first frost of October took the edge off the stench.

I doubt if the Gettysburg Chamber of Commerce was quite as thrilled at the prospect of battle as our own was, unless you considered the members who were undertakers or bone collectors. Well, I wasn't there to provide social criticism; I was there to make sure things went off smoothly and that everyone got home safe after leaving all their money at local businesses. At 10 a.m., it was time for the safety briefing from the back of the flatbed truck that had hauled in the port-a-potties. Not exactly a heroic platform, but very practical. Looking out over the crowd of reenactors, I was struck by how outnumbered the Yankees were. If the South had enjoyed a similar ratio during the actual war, they would be singing "The Bonnie Blue Flag" at the World Series. Both sides still had their colors cased, and drummer boys pecked out rhythms as formations began to take shape. The number of horses had doubled since last year; forty-seven mounted reenactors had registered for the event. Divided into two roughly equal groups, the mock cavalry sat at the rear of my audience.

Most of them had gone to a great deal of trouble to be as authentic as possible. The overwhelming majority of Rebs wore homespun wool, dyed with the extract of walnut hulls into a soft khaki color known as butternut. Other than the color they were, there were more multi-forms than uniforms. Standing in loosely aligned ranks, they resembled an old-time chain gang, more than anything else. The Yankee reenactors were, of course, considerably better equipped and knew how to stand in a straight line. Dressed in sweaty-looking dark wool uniforms fronted with shiny brass buttons, most also wore clumsy hobnailed shoes that must have been a living hell to break in. All of them carried heavy muskets, and many wore bulky leather packs or wool blanket rolls slung over their shoulders, plus a wide assortment of canteens, binoculars, and cartridge pouches. I could even spy the grips of a couple of contraband bowie knives. This year they had brought a contingent all the way from Iowa. The newcomers wore baggy red pants, short embroidered waistcoats, and felt hats shaped like flowerpots — honest-to-gosh Zouaves. Every face turned toward me was already shining with sweat; here and there a man could be seen sucking on a wooden or metal canteen. There were plenty of anachronistic touches here and there: the odd wristwatch and very modern eyeglasses.

At 10:15 a.m., I cranked up the megaphone and proceeded with the safety lecture. "Good morning, everyone, and welcome to the third annual reenactment of the Battle of New Garnett. I'll be brief so everyone has time to get into position. I'm Detective Dewy Law and will be acting as the chief safety officer."

I held up a triangular red flag stapled to a wooden dowel about three feet long. "We have a few changes this year and I'll explain them briefly. Every safety officer will have a flag like this one I have here. When you see someone waving the red flag, you are to immediately cease fire and ground your weapons."

In the other hand, I waved around a green flag. "The green flag means you may proceed with the show. When you see green you may proceed with the battle; when you see the red flag everyone will cease fire, clear?"

Everyone nodded but there were a few faces on both sides that looked a little confused. So far, so good.

"Officers, I want you to make sure that the battle lines come no closer than one hundred yards to each other. The limits are marked by a line of red chalk that's hard to miss. Now, last year there were several folks who got so excited they forgot to remove their ramrods before shooting. One almost speared a young lad in the role of drummer boy, so keep your distance and careful with those ramrods, all right? If anyone here actually gets hurt, the liability insurance will go through the roof and the city will have to cancel next year. Everyone got that?"

A small rumble of response. "Mighty fine. Look, one more thing. I can spot more than a few knives and daggers out there, and I'd really appreciate it if ya'll would take them back to your cars and lock them in the trunk. I know they carried them back in the good old days, but we're not here to really spill blood today. We're here to just have a good time."

Another round of nods but they didn't strike me as terribly sincere about the subject of safety. I couldn't stifle the nagging voice telling me there was some genuine hostility out there. They were beginning to fidget like antsy kids, but I didn't let them go quite yet. There remained the most important matter to bring to everyone's attention. "One of the complaints we had last year was reenactors relieving themselves in the woods. We've brought in more toilets this year so that shouldn't be an issue this time around. Everyone got that?"

There was a shouted answer from the neat Yankee ranks. "That was the Rebs crapping in the woods! Just like they do at home!"

This comment was followed by a chorus of outraged denials from the milling mob of Southerners. The Yanks responded with more degrading comments about the sanitary habits of their ancient enemies. I had to turn the bullhorn's volume up another click to regain control.

"All right, all right, doesn't matter who did it last year, but don't do it this time around. If you gotta go you'll have a chance. The first show is scheduled to kick off at 11 a.m. and the second will be at 4 p.m. Now I want everyone to have fun and put on a good performance for the audience. Any more comments or questions?"

A potbellied Yankee officer raised one finger, and I nodded at him in recognition. "Mr. Law, there's a lot of nearlys in the Rebel ranks. Do we have to fight them too?"

Another shower of verbal abuse erupted from the Southerners mixed with Yankee laughter, but I wasn't sure why. I walked to the edge of the truck bed. "I'm sorry, sir, what do you mean by … nearlys?"

He pointed at a youngish man standing in the front of the Rebel ranks. "That boy there is wearing sneakers! People didn't wear sneakers in the Civil War! He's not completely authentic, just nearly. And look at that fellow over there. He's wearing an Atlanta Braves baseball cap for crying out loud."

The boy wearing the Braves cap responded before I had a chance to. "Hey, Billy Yank, there weren't any fat asses back then either, but they let you in!"

Torrents of laughter colored with an undertow of genuine hostility. Well, at least it wasn't going to be hard to make them fight; the challenge would be to make them hold off until show time. The Yankee captain scowled and grumbled but held his piece. I decided the quicker I finished, the less chance there would be for actual violence to break out.

"One last thing. As you've all seen this year, we have some artillery, or rather the Rebs do. I want to compliment my old friend

Larry Lewis and his pals for the dead-on reproduction they did on a model 1841 six-pounder cannon. It's an exact copy of New Garnett's own legendary gun known as the Bulldog. It wasn't cheap, and they put in a lot of work to get it finished in time. Let's have a big hand for Colonel Larry Lewis and the New Garnett artillery!"

The Rebs cut loose with their signature yell, and the Yanks pouted and grudged a little halfhearted applause that was drowned out by their opponents. The exotic, corn-fed Zouaves stood like inexpressive circus mannequins, but I could see what they were thinking: 'Next year we'll have a pair of cannons and they'll be twice as big.'

"All right, everyone, it's an hour til show time, so there's plenty of time to hit the bathrooms and write that last letter home. Larry … uh, Colonel Lewis, I want to see you and your crew for a few moments. Please remember, you see that red flag and everyone stops shooting immediately. Any more questions? No? Good deal. Dismissed. Everyone be safe and have fun!"

Orders were shouted and the Yanks marched off smartly in lock step, led by the Zouaves. The Rebel ranks trailed behind the Yankees, when, over the outraged protests of the other side, several mock Confederate soldiers dashed ahead to grab the best seats. More men sprinted ahead and the neat blue ranks dissolved in the rush to the toilets. The Iowa detachment remained in step, a lonely line of men wearing bright red pants, quaint hats, and white spats, following the mob like a troop of heavily armed bellhops.

Larry and his crew came over to the truck as I climbed down. It gets harder and harder to reconcile those high school faces with the current version as time slips past, but his eyes were just the same, audacious and courageous, in a stupid kind of way. We shook hands all around. He had a half dozen strange faces dripping with that peculiar coastal accent. The gun crew, all employees of Lewis Shipbreaking and Scrap, had been recruited from the distant wastelands of lower Mississippi.

"Hello there, Larry, how's things down in Pascagoula?"

"Fine, Dewy, just fine. Things are slowing down a little bit. You'd think after this long, every Navy ship in the world would have been broken up, but we got enough coming in to keep the lights on."

He aimed a bony finger tipped with a half-black nail across the field. “So what do you think of the new Bulldog?”

I nodded. “It’s mighty fine, Larry. That’s a dead-on full-scale reproduction, but there’s something I want to mention to you fellas. I got some disturbing reports of a live fire practice in a remote gravel pit last weekend. Boys, has anything like that been going on out there?”

Pale faces and nervous glances all around. Larry had worn the same expression when he got caught cheating on an Algebra exam only twenty-five years ago. That was all I needed to establish probable cause. “Damn boys, I could run you in for that! Those are federal charges if they catch wind of it! What the hell were you thinking?”

Larry shrugged. “We just wanted to see if we could hit anything. All we did was shoot up some old cars. No harm done.”

I shook my head. “You get caught by the feds and I won’t be able to help you. I hope you didn’t bring any live ammo. What were you shooting with it?”

Larry took on a matter-of-fact tone. “I collected a pile of ball bearings from an old Russian aircraft carrier we junked out. They fit the new Bulldog like a glove. Seemed a shame just to melt them down. Honest, Dewy, we shot off all we had down at the gravel pit. We got nothing with us but blanks. Come on now, Dewy, we both know of a person that’s done a lot worse, right?”

He still wore the same cagey look he wore when cheating on tests or milking government contracts, right down to the last dime. I couldn’t decide what to do. People would be upset if I took him in now, and if I let him go, he’d do it again for sure. Above all, I couldn’t take the chance he would rat me out. He could make a lot of trouble. Turned out, I didn’t have to decide that very second, because a small disturbance had broken out at the toilets.

A swirling melee had spontaneously erupted in front of one of the portable potties. I could see fists flying above a tight circle of cheering onlookers who shouted encouragement to the combatants. A couple of New Garnett’s finest had arrived on the scene about the same moment under a deluge of boos and catcalls. The Rebel who wore tennis shoes had been mixing it up with a couple of Zouaves. I was pretty annoyed. Everything had been going so well; you'd think they could have waited for the battle.

The boys held them back, and I put on my "tough cop" hat. "All right, guys, what the hell is all this about?"

One of the now fez-less Iowa Zouaves, a tall, sandy-haired man with a drooping moustache, pointed an accusing finger at the battered Rebel. I noticed his knuckles were skinned. "That man cut in front of us! We waited in line and so can he!"

Compared to the natty Zouaves, the Rebel looked like a hobo dressed in mismatched third-hand military clothing. He was a dried-up little guy with a pinched face and buck teeth, but he made up for his lack of size and looks with a badgerish attitude. The mock soldier observed me with a contrite expression. I didn't know him. His accent was a lot more East Texas than North Alabama. All of them came a long way just to have a fistfight.

"They was hoggin' up the privy! When I got to go, I got to go! When I come out, they up and jumped on me, just out of the blue!"

Decisions, decisions. This was getting to be a little too much trouble. I decided the main thing was to get on with the show, then both sides could work it out of their systems. I wouldn't dare shut things down over a schoolyard brawl, but they didn't know that.

"Any more bullshit like this and I'll run all your sorry asses in! Now stay out of trouble!"

The delinquent Iowa boys were collected by their own, and the scrappy Rebel was scooped up by a group of friends, who, as I had correctly guessed, had come all the way from Texarkana. It took a little longer than planned for both sides to assemble. The sun climbed higher and the day took on the penetrating warmth of early spring. The slopes overlooking the mock battleground were covered with lawn chairs, bright plastic coolers, and picnic lunches spread on old blankets. I looked at my Timex: 10:45 a.m. Thank providence.

A few minutes later, I was between the opposing forces, checking in by radio with the other safety officers on either end of the line. The Yanks were so outnumbered, the Rebel line overlapped theirs by a good twenty-five yards on both ends, something that had happened rarely, if ever at all, in the war. After a good deal of sweaty effort, Larry and his crew had wheeled the golden cannon up to the far end of the Rebel line by hand. I gave him a wary look, and he just smiled and waved. The minutes dwindled down.

The mayor walked between the lines holding a chromed microphone attached to a long black cord that snaked back to his trademark red Cadillac, topped with four large speakers — an arrangement that usually came out only at election time. I scanned the crowd of tourists for Planter or any other suspicious characters. The cannon still nagged at me, but I forced myself to put it aside. I hadn't seen any live ammo in their kit, and I really didn't have any reason to believe that Larry would have been stupid enough to bring any. I hadn't seen any government trucks since the Gort ran Vanzetti and his crew out of town, but that didn't mean they weren't here.

"Good morning, everyone, I'm Mayor Vernon Sanders, and I want to welcome you all on behalf of the citizens of New Garnett and the New Garnett Chamber of Commerce. We're here today to observe the terrible battle and sacrifice made by both sides during the Battle of Garnett on April 1, 1865. It was a hard-fought battle that was the last Confederate victory of the War Between the States! Remember, everything at Bell-Huckson's department store is ten percent off today! Housewares, appliances and clothing, you name it and they got it! And remember, everything is on sale!"

With that dramatic revelation, the Yanks gave each other puzzled looks, and a howling cheer went up from the Southerners. I was a little confused myself; everything I had ever read or heard indicated a brutal last-ditch fight that left the town in ashes and the town's garrison practically eradicated. The mayor continued his welcoming speech. If he was aware of any glaring historical inaccuracies, he didn't let on.

"I want to remind everyone to remain behind the white police tape for your safety. Those are real guns out there, and even without bullets, they can inflict a nasty burn or even bust an eardrum! All right, mighty fine! Everyone remember to shop New Garnett's downtown, and don't miss the big bluegrass show at the Buckin' Bronco Arena tonight! Thank you for comin'!"

I thanked the mayor and checked with both safety officers by hand radio; it was 11:00 a.m., time for kick-off. The casings had come off the flags of both sides, and for a few moments, there was just enough of a breeze to bring them to life. On the Northern side: several large Stars and Stripes were grouped with a cluster of state flags, all gallantly streaming. On the Southern side: most were flying the venerable and sometimes reviled Stars and Bars. There was a new one this year — a copy of the last official flag of a failed nation that couldn't decide how to do anything but argue. The familiar Stars and Bars had been shrunken to a small reservation in the upper corner on a field of pure white. It's like the committee that had approved it had wanted to surrender but couldn't quite bring themselves to it. It was the only battle flag in history that announced that the people waving it were really giving serious thought to throwing in the towel. Maybe they thought it would make defeat easier to bear, like getting into a hot bath a little bit at a time.

I blew the whistle, waved my own absurdly small red flag, and ran like hell for the sidelines. I was thinking both sides would wait until I got clear; I don't know where I got that idea. A rippling roar of harmless musketry from both sides drove me flat on the ground out of pure instinct. The Zouaves had dashed out of the battle line and fired so quickly and so close, my ears were ringing like church bells, and I had to pat out glowing fragments of cartridge paper clinging to my jacket. I toyed with the idea of red-flagging the nearest offenders, but one look around told me that was only an exercise in futility. All up and down the lines, men were working ramrods like angry kids churning butter. Scrambling to my feet, I dashed out from between the combatants as new volleys blasted billowing clouds of grey smoke into the warm spring air.

By the third volley, both antagonists had vanished under a sulfurous haze, but a thump that shook your heart on its moorings told me the new Bulldog had swung into action on the far side of the line. The crowd's bellowing approval could be heard between increasingly ragged volleys. The Bulldog barked again. Its flash could be seen through the murky haze-like lighting behind the fog. Coordinated fire began to deteriorate on both sides as every man began to load and shoot at his own pace. Someone handed me a coke in a paper cup, and I drained it in one long gulp, then consulted my wristwatch. They had been at it for only three minutes. At the rate everyone was burning through ammunition, the show wouldn't last more than a quarter-hour. Yanks and Rebels alike were using up cheap black powder like a gang of twelve-year-old boys on the Fourth of July.

An additional thump told me the Bulldog was still spitting fire. Getting down on one knee, I could peer under the haze, and what I found was disturbing: a neat line of red pants was a lot closer to the enemy than authorized by the rules of engagement. The drab Rebel colors were harder to spot but you could also catch disembodied legs breaking away from their own group to close with the Iowa boys. I decided to let it go, for now. They had to be getting low on ammunition and I could jack up both sides during lunch. I studied the mock causalities scattered on the ground. It was easy to see they were all just shamming, and there was none of the flailing around or eerily motionless shock that comes with a serious injury. Then I heard the real thing: a piercing scream followed by the savage laughter of approval cutting through the racket. I squatted down lower to peep under the smoke and spotted a small man on the ground. Both his hands clenched at a thick wire wrapped around his neck as his legs thrashed around like a fish at the bottom of a boat. Some idiot, intentionally or accidently, had fired off a ramrod that had wrapped around the man's neck like a hot python. I suspected it was no accident, but being a cop, I suspect everyone.

I blew hard on the whistle and brandished the red flag like I was waving off a botched landing. It had no discernible effect on either side, and both kept loading and firing as fast as possible. I looked again at their real casualty, and this time I realized it was the scrappy little fellow from Texarkana now being dragged back into friendly lines by friends. Another pair of men fell to the ground; it was one of those damned Zouaves locking horns with a Rebel who was undoubtedly from Texas. That was it. I didn't care if it was a Civil War battle; I just couldn't stand by and let two of the combatants strangle each other.

There was a brief lull in the firing, and I took the opportunity to dash between the lines, manically blowing my whistle and waving the little red pennant. The gunfire began to dwindle all along the line. I found Texarkana with a livid bruise wrapped around his face, propped up by a friend who was pressing a small silver flask to his bloody lips. The man was hurt, and it was time to call the medics.

I keyed the radio and was rewarded by a soaring metallic screech that came bursting out of the tiny speaker with so much force, I threw it down by reflex. A shout of alarm began to spread from the area where I had just come from, and I walked back out between the lines expecting to find another pocket of trouble. I was immediately knocked flat by a riderless horse galloping for all it was worth, leaving a trail of terror-generated manure behind. I was halfway to my feet when a crowd of fleeing men tumbled me right back down, where I landed on a pile of freshly laid horse apples. I jumped up, mad enough to handcuff the entire event, only to find myself alone, face-to-belly with the Gort. Its visor was open, and a small white star danced in the black void. Without thinking, I threw myself to one side.

I had felt the power before, and now I was feeling it again. Probably the only human who had lived through the experience twice. The hair-thin beam leaped out of its head and raced across the broad field to connect with a tall, ghostly sycamore about three hundred yards away. Impacting at mid-trunk, the glow spread up the tree to envelop every branch, twig, and tender new leaf in a light so intense I had to shield my eyes with manure-stained hands. When I blinked away the dancing blue dots, I could see the tree was gone. Not even a stump remained. The robot's visor slid quietly back down into the closed position, and I looked around to make sure everyone had gotten clear. Abandoned picnics were spread on the hillsides. A few terrified horses bucked and galloped in mindless circles as their owners struggled to bring them under control. A cloud of dust could be seen rising from the parking lot as families and reenactors from both sides fled the scene. The Gort was as serene as Stone Mountain, Georgia.

I can't prove that it was listening to me, but I know it was. After all, we were old friends. "Gort, ole buddy, I don't think Wyatt Earp could have cleared out this field that fast."

The robot said and did nothing. I walked around behind it to make sure it was ours. It was. The metal-flake purple paint was as brilliant as the day I sprayed it on its wide silver ass. I patted the Gort on the flank like a friendly old dog. "Thanks for taking it easy on them, Gort. I think they've learned their lesson."

I pondered the mystery of how it had gotten here and how it would get back before finally deciding it could take care of itself. I began to walk back toward the parking lot, looking forward to a hot shower to wash away the barnyard stink, when a motion at the far end of the field caught my eye. It was Larry and the Mississippi boys wheeling the Bulldog around to face the Gort. A red pickup truck bounced across the field, stopping in a shower of dirt. The tailgate slammed down, and a wooden crate tumbled out to burst open on the ground. Small black spheres rolled away from the shattered box.

Larry and his boys began to work the gun; it was obvious they were going to take a shot at the robot. I could hear his words drift across the field. "Target to the front! Solid shot! Range … two hundred yards!"

My heart dropped out of my butt and landed hard. Larry and his ship-breakers were going to have a poke at the Gort. I had smelled alcohol when I had counseled them earlier, but they were still pretty steady on their feet, so I had let the matter go. Like they say: no good deed goes unpunished. I heard the ethereal humming behind me and quickly saw that my worst fears were being realized. The robot's visor had opened and the light was beginning to dance back and forth.

I stood in front of the Gort, waving my puny red flag as I frantically searched for my whistle.

More words, volume softened by distance, but none of the urgency was lost. "Clear the gun! Prick the powder bag!"

One of the crew had already removed the beefy wooden pole used to ram the charge home. Another man fiddled with the gun's touch hole as Larry studied us through period reproduction binoculars. I swore to myself that I would weld the cage door shut when I got my hands on them, provided any of us lived to see the sunset.

I shouted with every ounce of strength. "Larry! Don't you dare fire that damn gun!"

The idiots ignored me. "Fuse the gun!"

Larry was eating it up. Drawing his sword, he took the same heroic pose you see frequently depicted by battlefield monuments across the South, but would have marked you for instant death in the real thing. I saw one of the gunners planting something into the back of the gun and unrolling a length of line away from it — a friction fuse and lanyard. I dashed to one side and threw myself down, for some inane reason. Pure instinct, I guess. I shouted a pointless and unnecessary warning at the robot. "Look out, Gort! Hit the deck!"

The light in the robot's head was jumping like a frog on a hot skillet. It was going to shoot any second now, but the awful word I had dreaded came across the field first.

"Fire!"

There was a deep low-frequency crash felt way down in the chest, and I saw something I had read about often but never quite believed. The black ball could actually be seen, in car-wreck slow motion, leaving the muzzle of the gun, contrasted against a giant puff of dirty white smoke.

I had been right about the range; the ball plowed into the earth a good fifty yards short of the target. My relief was instantly quashed by a piercing clang and the sight of the round leaping back up out of the earth. Either by luck, or far more unlikely, deliberate calculation, the ball had bounced off a hidden shelf of rock and was hurtling toward us like a line drive. I flopped back just in time to hear the sizzling roar of the ball pass overhead and watch it smack right through the robot's open visor to vanish inside its head.

The giant alien machine didn't react at all. From where I sat, it was plain to see the deadly light had been extinguished. The Gort looked about as lively now as a garbage can. Forgetting about Larry and his lethal toy, I got to my feet and slowly approached the Gort, then stood on tiptoe trying to get a better look into its head. I was still three or four feet from visor level, but I could see into the bottomless blackness inside. A single bit of down drifted out of the sky and floated into the robot's head. I looked closer, and when I got the light just right, motes of dust and pollen could be seen streaming into the void. When I knocked gently on the machine's belly, it boomed like an empty oil drum. "Hey, Gort, you all right?"

The robot did not answer. Its open head continued to sweep dust and bits of spent powder out of the air. Now I was really worried; Planter's words haunted my inner ear: 'The Gorts are immortal and indestructible; they can pass through the heart of a star unharmed.'

Another bit of information for the dossier: Planter had been wrong; the machine had been bested by a solid steel ball shot right between what passed for eyes. A million worries and fears began to flood my mind. Could it be repaired? Could we cover up the fact that it had been disabled by an antique cannon firing a six-pound ball of steel salvaged from an obsolete ship? How could you repair something that couldn't be damaged or destroyed in the first place? I pounded desperately on the brushed silver torso with one bare fist, and it echoed like a steel drum.

"Gort! You all right, hoss? Come on, buddy, say something!"

I heard a familiar voice behind me. "Good morning, Dewy. If it says anything, it'll be the first time one has ever done so."

It was Planter, wearing the same drab suit and watching me with the penetrating hazel eyes. I turned to face the alien representative and glanced down-range. Larry and his crew already had the gun hitched to the back of the pickup and were bouncing toward the parking lot. They had left behind a scattering of solid shot, the giant ramrod, and an overturned wooden bucket. I made a solemn promise to myself to get warrants for Larry and every damn one of the Bulldog's crew. I nursed the faint hope that if we turned the vandals over to Planter and his people, things could be smoothed over before the feds got involved. I grasped for something to say like a drowning man grabs at the same water that's going to kill him.

"Mr. Planter I want you to know that the town of New Garnett is required by law to carry liability insurance … uh … we're obliged to pay for … uh … repairs … or replacements. We'll be happy to put up the deductible."

He ran a manicured hand across the robot's arm like someone examining their new Cadillac after a fender bender. He spoke aloud, mostly to himself. "This can happen only on the impossible planet." He sighed in exasperation. "What are we going to do with you people?"

In desperation, I blurted out the secret that I alone, out of seven billion human beings, had carried with me for thirty years. "Can't we find another star to power it with? You know, like a new battery?"

Planter covered his mouth in shock and then took a quick look around; people were beginning to meander in our direction but were still out of earshot. "Dewy! How did you come by that knowledge? No one knows about that but the Permanent Peace!"

I cast my eyes toward the ground and shuffled my feet. "Worked it out a long time ago, on the night that I, uh, painted Gort's butt."

The hazel eyes were wide with disbelief. This was really interesting, and it was a rare thing to see any emotion at all from one of them, besides a polite smile. "What? It was you?"

I spread my hands and indulged in a sheepish little grin. "I was just a kid. Seemed like a fun thing to do at the time."

He looked at the inert robot and then back at me. "How then are you still here? Why didn't it attack you?"

"Well, yes sir, in a way it did. It blasted the paint can and a pack I had dropped. But it didn't harm me at all, just scared the living piss out of me. That's when I got a good look in its noggin and well, I just knew, that's all. There was something about the light that reminded me of the stars on a clear night, and I just made the connection. Just call it good detective work. I'm sorry, Mr. Planter, it was just a youthful indiscretion."

People were beginning to edge closer with a little less fear now. Planter lowered his voice. "Dewy, you must never speak of this to anyone! If this became general knowledge, I could not guarantee your safety!"

I shrugged. "Mr. Planter if you learn one thing on your mission here, it should be this: on planet Earth, no one's safety is ever guaranteed. No one, and I mean no one — from the Secretary-General of the UN on down to the most ignorant backwoods hillbilly — has a guarantee of anything except death and taxes."

Now a crowd was gathering around us, but it didn't seem to matter who heard him anymore. "How can you, how can anyone live like that? The uncertainty of your lives, the constant threat of a mass extinction hanging over your heads every second of your existence. Its … its … "

"Impossible? Not really. You can get used to anything. Look at ole Blind Bill, he probably was only seventeen or eighteen when poison hooch fried his eyes out, but he went on with his life, has a nice family, and comes to work five days a week. You know, it's Blind Bill who took it on himself to polish up the Gort. Does every bit by feel and memory. No, Mr. Planter, it's not impossible to live here. I don't know if this makes any sense, but it's impossible not to. If anything, it makes life all the more sweeter."

He winced like he had bitten down on a bad tooth, squinted his eyes, then rubbed both temples with his forefingers.

"Say, Mr. Planter, do you feel all right?"

He shook his head. "I have an unusual discomfort in my head. It's like someone has put my skull into an industrial press."

"It's called a headache. It's usually brought about by a stressful situation, but it might just be allergies. Come on back to the office and I'll get you a BC powder. It's a native remedy, and I promise it'll take the edge off."

He nodded then looked up at the inert machine. "What about the Gort?"

I smiled. "What about it? I doubt if anyone's going to steal a ten-foot-tall alien robot."

He gave me the knowing look of someone made cynical by repeated disappointment. "I guess you're right. We shouldn't just leave it here. Somebody might try to do something crazy with it." His voice dripped with very real sarcasm.

"Don't you folks have some sort of recovery service?"

Now he actually looked like someone at the end of his rope. "No, we've never needed one until today."

"Tell you what, if you're really worried about it, I'll call Callie's Wrecker Service and we'll take the big rascal back to town with us. So, how much do you think that big fella weighs?"

Turned out, it didn't weigh more than a couple strong men couldn't handle. It took some convincing, but I reminded Callie that even tow truck operators were obliged to cooperate with the Permanent Peace, and it wasn't long until we had the Gort chained down on the truck like a small silver whale. By the time we got back to New Garnett, word had gotten around and the roads were lined with smiling, cheering people. Back at the courthouse, we were greeted by throngs of people acting like we had won the SEC championship.

The Gort was carried back to his little flower garden like a triumphant coach, standing him on his boxy feet in the same exact spot where he had been when I painted his ass decades ago.

We cheered and clapped. The crowd fell into an awed silence when Blind Bill tapped his way out to his friend with a cardboard box tucked under one arm. Bill gently felt the robot's surface with fingers made sensitive by a lifetime of darkness. I thought I saw him whisper something to the robot, although I couldn't hear what it was. He then pawed around in the box and came out with a can of Tortoise brand car finish and an old sponge, then began to tenderly apply the wax. The next thing I knew someone had brought out a ladder, and dozens of people were competing to give the Gort the polish of its life from head to toe. Bluegrass musicians began to tune up as people spread blankets on the lawn and light up portable grills to cook hotdogs and hamburgers.

Planter and I watched the street party from my window. He smiled as squealing children chased each other around the Gort's massive feet and swung like crazed monkeys from its half-clenched hands. It was also the first time I had seen the Black and white residents of New Garnett mingle with genuine friendliness. I know that all the hurts, insults, and misunderstandings of a hundred years couldn't be wiped away in a single night, but I think we made a fair start. Planter drank enough coffee to wake Shady Rest Cemetery, but never had to go to the can once. The party was almost over when he took his leave, but not before asking me if we had plans for the Gort.

"Well, I'll have to clear it with the city council, but I reckon we'll have to anchor him down so he doesn't take off like a cheap house trailer the next time a tornado comes through. Next council meeting, I'm going to propose we celebrate every April first as the Gort's birthday. Yeah, yeah, I know, you have no idea how old it really is, but we'll throw it a birthday party anyway. Before you go, I do have one more question, if you don't mind?"

By now, Planter's eyes had the jumpy glaze of too much caffeine, but it seemed like he felt better. It took some convincing to get the BC powder in him, and much to his amazement, the stuff had worked. "Sure, Dewy, shoot."

I smiled. I could see this boy had a good future as the Permanent Peace's go-to man for Earth relations. "Do you think it will ever reactivate?"

Planter shrugged, got up, and walked to the office door. For a moment I thought he was going to leave without answering, but he stopped and turned to nail me down with those penetrating eyes. "Who can say, Dewy? There's only one thing I know for sure: this is the impossible planet where anything can happen, even the impossible. Good luck, Dewy, and keep that token I gave you close at hand. You never know when it might be useful."

I nodded. "Sure thing. It saved my bacon for sure when the feds were here. I wish there was something just as valuable I could give you."

Planter reached into his pocket and held up the medicine bullet between his thumb and forefinger. "You already have, Dewy. I'll see you this fall and we'll take that trip … to the woods? I feel like I have a great deal left to learn, and you are the man to teach me. I know you'll take care of the Gort for us. I'll see you when the water begins to solidify. What is it you call that?"

"We call it the first frost."

"Yes, the first frost. I'll see you then. Be careful, Dewy, this is a dangerous place."

Then Planter placed the medicine bullet carefully in his pocket, walked into the darkened courthouse hall, and was gone.

THE END

Made in the USA
Monee, IL
27 September 2024